Zero to Ten:
Nursing on the Floor

Patricia Taylor

Livingston Press

The University of West Alabama

ISBN 13: 978-1-60489-310-6, hardcover
ISBN 13: 978-1-60489-309-0, trade paper
ISBN 13: 978-1-60489-311-3, e-book
Library of Congress Control Number: XXXXXXX
Printed on acid-free paper.
Printed in the United States of America by
Publishers Graphics
Hardcover binding by: Heckman Bindery
Typesetting and page layout: Cassidy Pedram
Proofreading: Christin Loehr, Keneshia Cook,
Kelley Roscoe, Brooke Barger
Cover art, design, and layout: McKenna Darley
Author photo: Amanda Nolin

Some of these stories were published in slightly different form in the following:

Red Dirt Forum

Healing Hearts

The Sucarnochee Review

Belles' Letters 1 and 2

Livingston Press is part of The University of West Alabama,
and thereby has non-profit status.
Donations are tax-deductible.

first edition
6 5 4 3 2 1

Zero to Ten:
Nursing on the Floor

Dedications

To my dad, Ron Willey, for taking me to the hospital to see patients when I was a child and for helping make my nursing career a reality.

To Ruth Ann Taaffe, my first and best nursing buddy.

To my dear "Scribbler" friends, Sarah Langcuster-Kleist, and Christen Loehr, for editorial advice, support and love.

To Suzanne Hudson for spending a great deal of time making insightful suggestions for this collection.

And to Joe Taylor. I couldn't possibly name the ways.

Table of Contents

FOREWORD

This mostly fictional story collection is based on experiences of being a registered nurse for 40 years in various settings and places in the southeast USA. One of the advantages of nursing is that one can change jobs and titles easily, especially with increased education, and so I took advantage of this in my career which is evident in this collection. Primarily I worked oncology nursing and hospice as well as some medical-surgical, emergency room, quality control and psychiatric nursing. And I had the opportunity to teach in an associate degree nursing program for 20 years which added to my experiences with patients. I was primarily a psychiatric instructor, but my role also involved taking students to a variety of other settings, which included obstetrics, pediatrics, long-term acute care, and long-term care nursing. These stories also include recollections of experiencing illness and death from a family's perspective which is a whole new thing.

These stories were written over a period of many years as an attempt to cope with the challenges of my career. The stories are just a sampling of many experiences with patients and families, but they were not written with a collection in mind, so their chronology is off. This foreword's purpose is to explain the discrepancies in the time periods.

The first story, "Something New," did not occur when I was in nursing school in 1974-6, but was a culmination of births while taking students to the O. B. unit in the 1990's and 2000's. It is the beginning of the narrator's story and a way to begin framing the collection. Likewise, the second story, "Till Death Do Us Part," is based on my students in the 1990s giving nursing home clients an experience of participating in a wedding and reminiscing about past occasions. It's also based on one exceptional elderly female friend. On the other hand, the third story, "The Promotion" was written with my memory of my first nursing job in 1977. While I still have memories of the horror of late trimester abortions, this is not written as a political or religious statement, but simply my observations and emotions at the time. Incidentally, the nurses, including myself, on that unit wrote letters to the administrator of that hospital to report what was happening and abortions were stopped at that hospital after I had left the unit.

The stories "Sex on The Beach," and "Zero to Ten" reflect my experiences working with cancer and AIDS patients (the funeral scene is based on a real event, as well as is the incident of the woman with the neck tumor) in the early to mid-1980s. "Nuances of Pain" is based on being with students on a pediatric unit in the 1990's."Just a Nurse" is a purely fictional account based on experiences working with students and patients on a long-term acute unit, on some observed mother-daughter dynamics, and on some attitudes about nursing as a career. The next two stories, "Wonderful Job on Dove Lane" and "Mama," are loosely fictional accounts of working for Hospice in the late 1980s and again demonstrate the difficulties of caring for family members as well as patients.

"I'll Fly Away," is my best recollection of my mother's cancer diagnosis and death in 1996, and my persistence to make sure she had a peaceful, comfortable experience with Hospice. And "Angels" is again an account of my experiences as an instructor working with students at a state psychiatric facility in mid 1990s when there was a great deal of room for a lot of people who needed help and the patients could roam the spacious grounds during the day, smoke cigarettes, and attend dance hops. But soon enough this ended when states started accepting only a minimal number of patients, allowing them to stay a

Patricia Taylor

very short time, and when accrediting agencies insisted patients stay inside most of the day to do "therapy," and when hospitals no longer allowed patients to smoke.

In 2011, I retired early from teaching to return to much missed bedside nursing. "The Quality Nurse" reflects my experiences working at a small rural hospital where I wore multiple 'hats,' including being a floor and ER nurse as well as Quality Control nurse. So this story represents me in all my roles. I admit I was making fun of my quality control role just a little, as I think this is how I was viewed by the other nursing staff.

My mother-in-law's illness and death are represented in "What She Wanted," and the story presents an accurate account of what happened in 1990. It again demonstrates my strong commitment to the Hospice philosophy.

"Enid, Ward Six," "One Lie Short," and "The One Who Gets the Hugs," are all based on my brief but overwhelmingly frustrating and rewarding career as a staff nurse in a state psychiatric hospital in 2011. The stories speak for themselves, but I still grieve that I was not able to continue this work and be a help to these clients who are in such need of support, tolerance, and kindness.

The narrator's story ends here, but I did go on to work at a very compassionate private geriatric psychiatric unit.

Thank you for reading. I really hope you enjoy this collection.

Patrica

Something New

"*J*ust stay here and offer yourself," says Mrs. T., my nursing instructor, as she blesses me with her crooked, exaggerated smile and bounces out of the birthing room. On the way down the hall, heading towards this room with her, I had told her I was scared. She had chirped, "Everything new is scary."

This is something new all right. It's our first day of O.B. clinical in the hospital. I'm dressed in scrub top and pants that are two different shades of faded green and are big enough to hold another person in them; the pants legs are rolled up several times and keep falling down. I feel very vulnerable, like I'm walking around in my tackiest p.j.'s from home. I no longer have the protection of my stiff white student uniform with the red stripe and school patch that make me feel important. And all we've studied so far in class are the signs and symptoms of a normal pregnancy. Certainly not anything to do with the scene before me now. I'm alone in the room with a beautiful young dark brown woman whom Mrs. T. just told me is in active labor. *Like, in going to have a baby.*

The woman is lying on her back with her head to one side and her eyes closed, her arms and legs limp. She has long braided hair that whips over her forehead and pillow. Her knees are bent and flopped to each side of her body with her belly protruding under a white sheet. She's wearing a bright blue hospital gown that has fallen off her shoulders and exposes the top part of her large breasts. A bag of clear intravenous fluid is flowing into a site on her right forearm.

Two long brown wires are hanging from under the right side of her sheet and hooked into a monitor that looks like a TV set. Wiggly lines run across the screen and a light that looks like a red heart is blinking along with numbers that change constantly but seem to stay between 145 to 150. The bed is shorter than usual, ending just below her feet.

I approach the right side of the bed slowly and then stop suddenly as the woman opens her eyes, grabs her belly, arches her back and starts to scream. I've never heard anyone scream like this before. I run to her and say, "What is it?"

"Lord have mercy," she murmurs between gritted teeth before she lets out another wrenching scream. I reach out to hold her hands, and she yells, "Don't touch me."

I think about running out to get Mrs. T. or a nurse. *But should I leave my patient? Mrs. T. wouldn't like that. Call the nurse?* I grab for the call light. But then the woman calms down as suddenly as she started up. Her limbs fall back to her sides and she lets out a relieved sigh. She looks at me as if for the first time and smiles.

"Hi. I'm Patti, a student nurse. I've been assigned to stay with you. Is that OK?" I'm afraid of what she will say.

"Sure, it's bad being alone," she says as she closes her eyes again. I inwardly sigh with relief. I didn't want to get kicked out of my first patient's room. "Can I have some water?" she asks weakly. I don't know if she is supposed to have anything to drink or not, but there is a cup of crushed ice with a spoon on the bedside table, so I scoop up a few small pieces and say, "Here's some ice." She opens her eyes and mouth as I spoon the ice into her mouth. She murmurs "Ummm," and chews on the ice, while I stand with the cup preparing to give her more.

"Oh Shit," she blurts out, raising her arms and knocking the cup out of my hand. The cup plummets over the side of the bed with ice scattering over the floor. Perspiration is popping up on her forehead and she's writhing back and forth holding her abdomen. She's hollering again, "God bless, God bless," and then starts with ear-shattering screams. She pulls at her gown roughly and reveals a large hard mass across her entire abdomen. *That must be the baby. How weird.* There are two straps across her belly to which the black cords I saw earlier are attached. I lean over her, tense and anxious to help, but afraid to touch her. When she stops rocking and screaming and pulling this time, I relax my whole body along with her and sit down on the stool beside her bed.

"I can't take much more of this," she moans as she relaxes back into the bed, legs sprawling with knees bent and arms loose again. *I don't know how much I can take either.* I see that her abdomen is no longer so tight and strained. One of the lines on the monitor beside her has made a large upside down u-curve. I go to her and pull down the gown and arrange the sheet neatly over her, and she smiles weakly. "How much longer will this be?" she asks. *As if I have a clue.*

"I don't know. Have you ever done this before?" I reply, hoping that she knows more than I do.

"Yes, four times. But it was never this bad before. I want this baby out!" She exclaims, adamantly pushing her braids behind her head.

"Yes, you seem pretty miserable," I say helpfully, remembering how Mrs. T. always stresses using empathy whenever possible. I wonder why she would be doing this for the fifth time if it was even half this bad before. I pat her hand and then leave her to go towards the bathroom to get a cool cloth for her wet, hot-looking forehead.

"Don't leave me," she blurts out as she tenses and starts to rock again. I run back to her just as a woman enters the room and walks up close to the bed beside me. I see her pink and blue scrubs and know she must be one of the nurses. I make out 'Carol' on her name tag. She is a petite brunette in her twenties; she looks a lot like me.

"Lakisha, take slow deep breaths like we practiced," Carol instructs her patient. *Lakisha.* I didn't think to ask for her name. Carol starts to model how Lakisha needs to breathe and I join in: deep breath, in through the nose, out through the mouth, faster as the contraction progresses, fast, fast, fast, then slow down, slow, slow, slow, deep cleansing breath, and relax. Lakisha takes a few breaths and then stops breathing with us and lets out sharp yelps between phrases of exasperation, "Lord have mercy." Carol keeps trying to get Lakisha to focus on breathing, but Lakisha won't do it.

When Lakisha does settle down she looks exhausted; her gown and sheets are rearranged again and her face is covered with perspiration. She just lies still with her eyes closed. "I don't know if I can do this."

Carol says, "Yes, you can," and then tells me to go ahead and get the cool washcloth. She helps Lakisha to turn to her left side. "The baby gets more oxygen this way," she says, cheerfully. She rubs lotion over her patient's back and straightens her sheets and gown. I put the wet cloth on Lakisha's forehead and then rinse off her face. She lies still again while Carol introduces herself to me and then helps me to understand what is going on.

"Patti, Lakisha is having uterine contractions that are forcing the baby into her pelvis. She's getting close to delivery. "She points at the TV-like monitor. "This lower line that looks like a lot of small hills is recording the contractions: They are doing just what they are supposed to do. And the top line is showing the baby's heart rate and how it is responding to each contraction." I notice again that the numbers read around 145.

Carol smiles at Lakisha, "The baby's taking the contractions well. If not, the heart rate would be dropping." *There's a lot more to this than I thought. In the movie it looks so quick, a few ladylike yelps and it's over.*

"What should I do?" I feel overwhelmed. *I hope I'm not responsible for monitoring any of this.*

"Just stay—" She doesn't finish the sentence because Lakisha starts to groan and balls up on her side around her large hard tummy.

"Damn," Lakisha blurts out. Carol takes my hand and shows me how I can massage Lakisha's lower back with lotion in slow rhythmic circles. I take over, and it does seem to calm her a little and she doesn't seem to mind me touching her there. She is calmer now that Carol is here too.

Carol goes to the other side of the bed and imitates correct breathing technique for Lakisha again while Lakisha seems to do her best to follow. I breathe along with them. Deep breath, in through the nose out through the mouth . . .

*   *   *

After the third go around of back rubbing from an awkward angle and deep breathing, my back and neck hurt and I feel dizzy. I want to cry out with Lakisha, *"How much longer?"* as she's done several times. Between contractions, we hear a soft knock and then the midwife comes in, smiling at Lakisha. I know it is the midwife because Mrs. T. introduced us earlier. She goes by the name of Judy and is attractive, 40-ish, with auburn hair. She wears blue scrubs and a spotless, starched white lab coat. Mrs. T had told me that Judy used to be a nurse on this unit and then went back to midwife school. I doubt that that is something I'd ever want to do. It is all too new, and strange, and scary.

Lakisha looks at Judy with great hope and expectancy, and Judy says, "I'm here to check you." Check what, I wonder. But Carol and Lakisha obviously know because Carol starts to help Lakisha roll over onto her back.

I must look confused because Carol tells me, "Judy's going to see how far Lakisha's cervix is dilated." I nod back, not sure what that means but I feel safer now that there are two experts here with us. I'll bet Lakisha does too.

Judy sits at the end of the bed, pulls the sheet up over Lakisha's knees, disclosing a large swollen vulva. She tugs a sterile glove onto her right hand and with her left hand she picks up a tube of lubricant and smears it over her right fingers. She tells Lakisha, "I'm just checking now," and inserts the first two fingers of her right hand into the vulva. Lakisha tenses a little but Judy reassures her by rubbing her left hand over Lakisha's abdomen, and saying "It will just be a minute."

Judy's right hand twists a little inside Lakisha and then Judy announces with a big smile, "You are at ten. It's time to start pushing." She just beams as she withdraws her hand. You'd think she just found gold. She leaves the sheet up over her patient's knees exposing all the lower part of her body. Lakisha doesn't seem to mind. I guess modesty doesn't mean much at this point.

"Thank God," sighs Lakisha, and then closes her eyes.

"Ten. What's that mean?" I bravely ask.

"Her cervix is completely dilated, it's open ten centimeters and big enough for the baby to be pushed out," Carol says to me. Then as Lakisha starts to tense with her next contraction, Carol tells her, "Lakisha, you need to push."

Lakisha arches her back, holds her breath, and pushes on the bed rails toward the foot of the bed. "Lakisha, don't hold your breath,"

Carol directs, but Lakisha only takes a big gulp and then holds her breath again. Judy washes her hands, and with one more encouraging smile she heads toward the door. *She can't be leaving. She can't be leaving.* And out the door she goes. I look back at Carol and Lakisha but they haven't seemed to notice Judy's departure; they are busy with Lakisha's contraction. *Why did Judy leave? Does that mean Carol might leave soon too? And leave me here alone with Lakisha?*

During the next break, Carol instructs Lakisha, "You're not going to get the baby out this way. You have to stop holding your breath, arching your back and pushing away from your body." Carol demonstrates in the air how to pull on the side rails towards her and to expel air like blowing out candles.

Lakisha watches her and says with angry tears, "I can't do that."

"Yes you can, you have to, Lakisha," Carol replies sternly now.

On the next contraction, Lakisha does the same wrong pushing again, though Carol is telling her what to do. It's almost as if Lakisha has decided to deal with this by being as rebellious as possible. She's like a two year old in Wal-Mart who won't come to her mother when she's called.

* * *

Two more contractions, and Lakisha looks weaker and is even more irritable. "I can't do this. You have to get the doctor and get this out." She has slipped down in the bed, her buttocks almost to the edge. The sheet has fallen on the floor and she barely still wears a gown. Carol looks between Lakisha's legs during every contraction and then looks disappointed. I guess she's looking for the baby. I'm at the end of the bed watching too. *Is the whole baby just going to come out on the floor? Shouldn't someone be there to catch it? Someone besides me?*

"Lakisha, if you just hang in there and push like I told you, it won't be that much longer. The way you are arching your back is just pushing the baby back up in to the birth canal," Carol explains with exasperated patience.

"I want you to get the doctor for surgery now," Lakisha insists loudly, and then another contraction hits her. She doesn't even seem to try to really push this time. She is holding her abdomen and crying out like she was before. When the pain stops she is adamant again "Damn it, I can't do this. I want this baby cut out **now**."

"Lakisha, you've done this before, you know you can," Carol reminds Lakisha which just seems to make her more angry.

"It's never been this bad before. I can't stand it. You have to get the doctor," she cries.

"If you had surgery, you'd have a lot more pain tomorrow than you ever thought about having now." Carol says in a calm but deliberate, low, voice. "Now watch me. You need to sit up and pull towards you. Then push down on your pelvis like you are going to have a bowel movement," she says as she holds out her arms and then brings her wrists and hands towards herself in demonstration.

"Would it help if she was up farther in the bed?" I ask, not sure if it is a good time to make any suggestions. She is lying flat and not really in a good position to push like she is having a bowel movement. *And the floor looks dangerously close to Lakisha's naked bottom.*

"Good idea, help me pull her up." Carol says. We both grab an arm and on the count of three pull Lakisha up while she pushes with her feet. Then Carol raises the head of the bed and positions Lakisha's hand on the end of the short side rails so that it would be easier for

Patricia Taylor

Lakisha to pull towards herself. I wipe her head again and say, "You can do this, the baby's so close." I don't know if this is true or not but it sounds encouraging to me.

Lakisha sighs, but with the next contraction she does pull up some and lean forward. Carol and I both take an arm and pull on it towards her body to remind her what to do. She takes a deep breath and pushes. "That's good, " we both groan with relief. It will be a real problem if she really can't push the baby out. I guess she would have to have surgery, which sounds scary.

When Lakisha rests again, her eyes close, and Carol seems to relax too and is in a lot better mood. She asks her patient, "Is the daddy here?" Lakisha nods her head silently. Carol continues, "Do you want Patti to go find him?"

"No, I never want to see his ass again," Lakisha pronounces severely, continuing to close her eyes. Carol smiles at me and I assume this is a common reaction of women in labor. Though if I ever have a child I'll expect my husband to be here suffering along with me. If he's present at conception he can darn well be at the delivery.

Carol checks the monitor strips and makes notes on a clip board as she's been doing all along. I sit on a swivel chair on the side of the bed feeling tired but too excited to rest. It doesn't seem possible that we are really waiting for a baby. It just seems like this will go on this way forever.

Judy comes back in, but Lakisha doesn't open her eyes until she sits up suddenly with the next big pain. Carol tells Judy, "It won't be long now." Judy uncovers the large sterile tray near the end of the bed, that has all the equipment she will need. She puts on gloves and a gown. Carol helps her to tie it in the back while I stay close to Lakisha and offer supportive words.

Another woman whom I haven't seen before walks in with

energetic steps, turns the lights on over a high table with plastic sides that has been up against the wall near Lakisha. She is Aretha Franklin dark with a Doris Day haircut. She stands behind Judy as if on call. Her name tag says 'Angelic.'

Judy sits on the stool at the foot of the bed and checks between Lakisha's legs. She says she is massaging the vulva to help prevent it from ripping during the birth. I peep to see what she is doing and see the vulva bulging and red from the pressure. *Rip? The skin can rip?*

Then Judy joins Carol and me to encourage Lakisha to push. "Push, push, push. . . . Hold it. Don't let go. Don't breathe. Don't breathe. Focus on your bottom. You are almost there."

Lakisha bends forward pulling on the armrests, holding her breath. Her face is bright red.

Suddenly another nurse with wild red hair runs into the room and screams at Judy," The woman next door is crowning now. You have to come." *Crowning?*

Judy seems to freeze a second. Then she turns to the redhead, "Couldn't you just make her pant until I can get there?"

"It ain't gonna happen," pronounces the wild redhead. *Do nurses talk like this?*

Carol says, "I'll work with Lakisha until you can get back."

"OK. Lakisha stop pushing till I get back," instructs Judy as she takes off her gloves and gown. *What? Stop pushing? Not push? After all we've been through?* I can tell from the horrified look on Lakisha's face that she is thinking the same thing.

Judy rushes off after the redheaded nurse. Angelic does the same, to leave the three of us alone again.

Lakisha's next contraction starts before she has time to say anything. Carol reminds her, "Don't push anymore right now. Just pant to slow down the baby until Judy gets back." She demonstrates for

Patricia Taylor

Lakisha again, this time panting, quickly in and out. Lakisha mimics the pant unenthusiastically at first, while glaring at Carol and me. I join in panting. *It's the least I can do.* We pick up the tempo and act like three large dogs after a long romp in the forest. Carol nervously checks between Lakisha's legs as we continue to pant throughout her contraction.

After two more attempts at panting, Lakisha is verbally angry again. "I can't do this anymore. I want this fucking baby out of me now. Get Judy or grab it yourself, it's coming," she pronounces. I can't say I blame her.

Sure enough, this time when Carol and I look down, not only is the vulva open, but there is a large dark mass edging out between the lips. "It's the baby's head," Carol says as she grabs the phone off the wall. Lakisha looks satisfied until the next contraction, and then she screams out and then sits up and pushes with all her might. Carol demands, "Don't push now," but Lakisha ignores her. I grab my hair and grit my teeth. *Is this what nursing is all about?*

Carol grabs the phone and yells into it, "We need Judy ASAP." I do know that this means, like *immediately.* After a pause she says, "She's crowning. We **can't** wait." She hangs up the phone, grabs a pair of sterile gloves and sits in the chair between Lakisha's legs. Lakisha starts to rest again and what is apparently hair recedes from view. Carol mumbles," Judy has just got the other one out and is cutting the cord. We have to wait a few minutes."

Carol implores Lakisha to pant and not to push next time. Lakisha has sunk back down to the end of the bed again, so it is harder for her to push, but she is also dangerously close to the floor once more. I assume it's not all that unusual for nurses to have to catch the baby, but Carol still looks nervous, like she'd rather not do this herself. I hope she doesn't have to either. Because for one, she looks real nervous, and for two I'll probably have to help.

Angelic trots in the room and stations herself near the high table. She puts a pink and a blue blanket and two small hats, one pink and one blue on the table under the lights. I guess she's going to help with the baby. That seems positive anyway.

Finally, Judy shows up. Carol jumps out of the chair and Lakisha cries out with relief.

Judy pronounces, "Now we're gonna get this baby out." Judy puts back on her sterile garb while Carol and I pull Lakisha back up in the bed and we each grab hold of a bent knee. Lakisha sits up and grabs hold of my hand. With the next pain, she pulls my hand backwards towards the rail. I'm in severe pain and my hand has turned white, but I'm not going to try to make a big deal of this. After all, a woman's having a baby. During the next rest I disengage my hand and massage it while I move to the end of the bed. I need to see what's going on anyway.

With the next contraction Lakisha gives one more big push and the baby's head comes sliding out.

"Thank You, Jesus! Praise God!" yells Lakisha.

I can't believe it's a baby's head, but there is hair and there are eyes, ears, and a little nose and mouth. I want to be happy, but the head looks so weird: it's pale and looks like it's covered in green hand lotion. It's not moving at all. And there is a lot of blood and green fluid coming from around it. Judy pronounces, "We have light meconium." I don't know what this means but in the movies there is no green fluid. Angelic hands Judy a clear plastic device with two tubes extending from it. One's short and the other's long and attached to a bottle on the wall. Carol whispers to me over the bed, "The baby has had a bowel movement because it is getting tired of pushing so long. It'll be OK. It's just important that it doesn't breath in the meconium."

Patricia Taylor

Judy sticks the small tube in the baby's mouth. With a sucking sound, greenish fluid is pulled back through the contraption and towards the bottle on the wall.

Then the body slips out behind the head. It's a girl. But she's all so pale and still not moving. Judy continues to pull fluid from each nostril. I'm scared. *Is she dead?* No one else seems particularly worried; they are just watching Judy with expectant expressions.

Sure enough, the baby suddenly starts to cry, a truly loud wonderful cry. And she starts to pink up. It's a little, pink, tense, moving *alive* baby. Everyone smiles and laughs and Judy holds the baby up for Lakisha to see, saying "It's a girl."

Lakisha is smiling now, calm, and laughing. Judy cuts the cord, and more blood spurts out. Then Angelic takes the baby and puts her under the warmer and dries her off, wraps her in the pink blanket, and places the pink hat on her little curly dark head. Then she hands the baby to Lakisha.

The mother holds the bundled baby up to her face, and says, "I love you, girl."

While Judy delivers the after-birth and cleans up, Lakisha turns to Carol. "Thanks Buddy," she says shyly. Carol smiles back and winks. I sit down.

This was just another routine event for Carol and the fifth time for Lakisha, but something mighty new for me. A few minutes ago I would have said that this was definitely not for me; it was all too much. Now I wonder. Maybe, just maybe, this is something I could get used to.

Till Death Do Us Part

*M*iss Mary watched with delight as the bouquet of multi-colored Walmart Christmas bows sailed into her lap. She held it up to her face, and grinned, questioningly, but with the assurance that something good had come to her. I hugged her thin soft shoulders and announced, "You caught the bouquet!"

"I did?" she replied as the wedding march music thrilled through the room and everyone else clapped for Miss Mary's good fortune.

*   *   *

It was the beginning of a new semester. And our instructor had announced that we would start with a month of geriatric nursing. We had all groaned, because that meant old people. We were going to be spending two days a week for the next month at the nursing home. I was pretty horrified and so were my fellow classmates. Most of us had some experience with a nursing home, not much, but just enough to know they were not joyful places. I remembered going with my church group every Easter through all of grade school to sing bunny songs and "Amazing Grace." We would huddle in the corner of the lobby while people in wheelchairs surrounded us. They looked so scary, like ghosts, and they smelled bad. They would try to touch us when it was time for us to walk among them and hand out plastic eggs. We would smile politely and move away as soon as possible.

And now, not only were we going back to visit, but we were actually expected to physically care for those people. "And you, Patti, are assigned to Mrs. Pratt, a ninety-two year-old female client with Rheumatoid arthritis, Osteoporosis, and Alzheimer's disease. She needs total care. You'll find her in 100." My instructor had calmly relayed this information to me, like it was really no big deal. Well, it wasn't – *to her.*

"Yes, Ma'am." I wrote down the information. I knew she expected me to meet my client, do an assessment of her problems and needs and then plan her care for the next month. She had already given us a brief tour of the facility and it was just like I remembered: dull green paint, halls lined with people in wheelchairs who wanted to touch me, and smells of body secretions. Not to mention loud crying from one of the rooms into which I could not see. Now I was on my own and headed for 100.

I found the room, the last one on the right, with a large straw hat decorated with pink flowers hanging on the closed door. A sign said in large letters, MARY PRATT, ROOM 100. I stood there a few minutes, dreading going in, but knowing I had to. Finally, I took a deep breath and knocked on the door. I heard a distant voice say "come in," so I pushed the door open and stepped carefully inside.

The room was bathed in color; blue and red and yellow poppies covered the curtains and bed. A quilt of multi colors spread over a chair and it was covered with yellow lacy pillows. She was sitting in a wheelchair by the bed in a bright purple robe with fuzzy hot-pink rabbit slippers. Sunlight streamed in on her from the window behind her and her white frizzy hair dazzled, like a halo. She was bent forward in her chair but I could see a large happy smile, which actually looked more like a scary grin.

All of this caught my attention, but I'm not sure that at the time I could have told you specifically what I saw. It was just an impression of *too much*. I didn't react right away, as I was confused and overwhelmed.

"Hi, Maude," she exclaimed, obviously excited to see me. I didn't know what to say. She thought I was someone else.

She reached out her crooked, swollen hands to me and jutted out her cheek. I bent down reluctantly and kissed her face. It was soft like velvet. And she smelled of Oil of Olay. It immediately brought back bad memories of an ex older boyfriend who used it every night to try to stay youthful.

Later, when I looked up rheumatoid arthritis, I found that this disease was what had caused her crooked and swollen joints and that it is a very painful disease. Also the Osteoporosis made her bones week, causing the very poor posture, and she was prone to fractures. As a matter of fact she had had several fractures.

But, at the time, I didn't know any of this. She told me to have a seat, which I did on the chair with the yellow pillows.

"How is your mother?" she asked pleasantly.

"She's fine . . . Mrs. Pratt . . ." I was trying to decide if I should tell her that she did not know me. We learned in class that it was best to 'present reality' when someone was confused.

"Call me Mary. You know me better than that." That smile again.

"Well actually, we just met. You might be confusing me with someone else. I'm Patti, a nursing student. I'll be visiting you for two mornings a week for the next month."

"We'll isn't that nice? It's nice to meet you, Patti. I just love nursing students." I felt relieved that she seemed to understand now who I was.

"Mrs. Pratt, I'd like to spend some time today getting to know you a little better." I had a long questionnaire I was supposed to fill out.

"Honey, call me Mary. And you already know all about me. I've known your mother for years and you too, since you were a little girl, Maude."

*   *   *

Normally it would take me several hours with Miss Mary (a compromise on what I should call her; my instructor's suggestion) to help her to bathe and dress, and eat. Everything took so long because she could barely do anything for herself, and it hurt her to be moved at all. I found out that it wasn't just her arms and hands that were twisted but her legs and feet too. She had to be lifted from the bed to the wheelchair because her old leg and hip fractures had healed but still caused a lot of pain and she was extremely weak.

Her mood continued to be cheerful, no matter what, even when she grimaced with pain, she would giggle and say, "That really aches." I'd think, *Get real already.* She was sweet, but so out of reality! And she kept calling me Maude.

For the first days, after I bathed her and helped her eat breakfast, I would just sit in her room with her until the morning was over. At first, this was the hardest time for me because I didn't know what to talk about. But I didn't need to worry about it because she'd talk on and on about the good times she had with Maude's mother and didn't seem to notice that I was not responding. I'd sit and plan what I would pick up to eat on the way back to class and then calculate how many hours I would need to study that night.

Nursing school was really challenging me. I flew through my prerequisites with all A's and now I was struggling to make a C, which was an 80% and mandatory to pass the course. When I wasn't working in the nursing home I was either in class or at home in my apartment studying or preparing a care plan the night before seeing Miss Mary. And that took me hours every time. Other students seemed to have time for fun activities like going to a movie or out to eat but I didn't think I had that luxury. I hadn't made any friends in school either because of that. I wanted to be a nurse since I was a little girl but I had no idea it was going to be so hard to reach that goal. I was starting to wonder if I could really do it. Maybe I wasn't real nurse material.

At the end of the clinical day, I would press my cheek to Miss Mary's powdered cheek and take another whiff of Oil of Olay. She'd say, "You were always such a sweet child, Maude." I'd think, *Right!*

*   *   *

It was our second week and our instructor told us that we had to plan an activity for all the nursing home clients. And, it needed to be something that would help the elderly people to reminisce about their lives. This had been shown to help confused people cope and connect with the present, she told us. Someone suggested that we put on a wedding. Another student told us his patient was an eighty-eight year old man who was living there with his wife. "They eloped sixty-nine years ago, and wouldn't it be neat to give them a real wedding now?" So it was decided.

To prepare the clients for the big event we were supposed to talk to them about their memories of weddings. I had never really asked Miss Mary much about herself and didn't expect to get much from her. When I had tried before, she had kept saying, "You know me." But I had to try to ask her questions again; my instructor would be checking on me.

Miss Mary was in her wheelchair, dressed in a long royal blue robe with her pink bunny slippers that were way too large, but were needed to cover crooked toes. She had insisted that I put bright make-up on her too; she loved color. I frankly thought she looked pretty silly, but she was so pleased with herself.

"Miss Mary. I need to tell you something. The nursing students are going to put on a wedding for some of the clients next week."

"Isn't that nice?" The smile got even bigger.

"Yes, and you are going to be invited." I leaned back in the chair and stuffed the yellow pillows up to give my aching back some support.

"Well, isn't that nice." *Duuhh*

"Will you tell me something about your own wedding?"

"My wedding? Well, really you should ask your mother. She was there." *Here we go.*

"I want to know what *you* remember."

"Well, my husband was a good man, I remember that." *Well, O.K.*

She sat there quietly and smiled, but seemed to be thinking too. Then I had a brainstorm, as my instructor would have called it. "Miss Mary, do you have any pictures of your husband?"

"Well, yes, somewhere. Why don't you look around and find them?" So I did. They were in a large photo album on the top shelf of the closet under some adult diapers.

I moved my chair close to hers and rolled her meal table over her lap. On it, I opened the black leather album. I helped her with her reading glasses (rainbow-colored, of course), and we both peered over to look at the pictures.

"Look, here I am with my daddy and my sisters." There was a black and white of a man in a coat and hat and three young curly-haired women in coats, hats, and gloves. "My mother died when I was a baby. But my daddy was wonderful. He took good care of us."

That shocked me. She grew up without a mother? I couldn't imagine such a thing. My mother was the most important person in my life. Although she was busy with four younger children and didn't have a lot of time to listen to me, I counted on her always being there in an emergency.

Miss Mary flipped the pages. They were covered with other black and white pictures of family when she was a young woman. Then there was one of her and a man; both were very young, and both were very solemn looking.

"That's Jack and me," She pointed. "On our honeymoon." They were both dressed in suits, hers with a skirt. They both wore hats; hers was jaunty over her right ear and with a feather. Wisps of curly light hair fell over her neck.

"Why do you both look so unhappy?" *Oops. I'd be in trouble if my teacher heard me say that. "Very un-therapeutic" she'd say.*

"That's how it was back then when you got your picture taken. You stood there so long in front of the camera while the photographer fooled with it that you forgot to smile." She laughed. "But, believe me, we were happy." She laughed again. Or rather, she giggled that time, and I could almost imagine a real blush under her fuchsia painted cheeks.

I suddenly realized that we were having a real conversation. And she made sense when she talked about the past. And it was the first time I saw that she was a real person, with a real life. She was someone's little girl, someone's sister, and someone's wife.

*   *   *

Patricia Taylor

"Miss Mary, you sure do like color." We were preparing for the wedding. She had insisted on a silky red dress, a double string of pearls, and gold and pearl *ear bobs* (as she called them). Also she chose a fuzzy knitted throw blanket made with every possible shade of blue to cover her legs and feet. I was putting on her red *rouge* (as she called it).

"Oh, yes, Maude. You know I've always liked color and to dress for fun. And when my daughter, Christina, put me in here, I made sure that she fixed the place up like I like it. And now when she visits she brings me all these pretty clothes." She touched her red dress and then stuck her lips forward for me to apply the crimson lipstick more evenly.

I had read on Miss Mary's chart that she didn't have any children. She had mentioned Christina before, and I thought it was someone from her past. I didn't realize that this might be an imaginary person. One of the nurses told me that she didn't have any regular visitors; her only family was a nephew that lived up north. He had come down and just moved her and a lot of her things into the home five years ago when she couldn't get around anymore.

"Miss Mary, I thought you didn't have any children." I gathered up the makeup supplies.

"Oh, no. Jack and I couldn't have children." She actually looked sad for a moment. "We wanted lots of children, but I lost three before they were born. Jack was so sad."

"Oh, I'm sorry." I couldn't imagine a life without children, I wanted to have several some day.

"And then Jack died too." Now, I *could* imagine a life without a husband. I hadn't had much luck with boyfriends. It's like a bumper sticker I saw once; "*Men are good for only one thing. But how often do you need to parallel park?*"

It was obvious, however, that this was not a happy prospect to Miss Mary. Her eyes actually misted up. I handed her a Kleenex and she dabbed her face, wiping off some of the newly applied powder.

"Well, we should get going to the wedding," I chirped. It was harder to deal with her sadness than her constant unrealistic cheerfulness.

"Oh, Maude, I need a hat," she suddenly exclaimed, back to her usual manner. I looked through her closet for a hat but found none. "I couldn't possibly go to a wedding without a hat."

I opened the door to her room, thinking I'd encourage her to go anyway, and I spied the straw hat decoration with the pink plastic flowers on the front of the door. I grabbed it. "How about this one, Miss Mary?"

"Oh, that is perfect. My daddy bought me that hat for my birthday." I doubted this, but I situated the hat cockily on her white curly head and escorted her to the wedding.

*   *   *

Miss Mary kept her bouquet of multicolored bows, along with the picture of her and her husband at their wedding, on the table by her bed at all times. I'd tell her how pretty she looked, and how wonderful that she caught the bridal bouquet. She'd say, "I did?" and smile. Her smile no longer looked scary, but had become glorious. And the Oil of Olay didn't smell so bad anymore either.

So I didn't quit going to visit Miss Mary when our month rotation of geriatrics was over. I found that I needed all that confused joy to help keep me focused on school. I started to see myself through Miss Mary's eyes; I was Maude who was a wonderful person and had always been such a sweet child. I took wonderfully good care of her,

Patricia Taylor

and obviously I could do the same with others. My grades were improving. I was smart, efficient, and organized and I was to become a nurse. I knew I would keep going to see her until death separated us. And actually even then, I could *still* be Maude if I wanted to be.

The Promotion

I am being ushered into the large, dark, inner sanctum of the Director of Nursing. She is a heavy imposing woman with an actual starched uniform and a large winged cap pinned to short straight hair; she looks like she may have once served in the Marines. You only get to see her on special occasions like this one. I was here one time before when I was first offered my job as graduate nurse three months ago. Since then, I have been doing all the things registered nurses do, with a lot of supervision from other nurses, but without a license.

But now is a proud moment for me. I just passed my licensing board exam, and I can wear a name tag that says, **R.N.** I am ready to accept my new full time assignment.

Mrs. Landsing tells me crisply, "Sit down." And before I am down, she starts again, "Congratulations on your achievement. We are very proud of you, and I have found you a perfect place to work."

I beam at her and marvel at my good luck.

"You will share the charge nurse position on 5-North Floor with your friend Ruth Allen."

*More good news. Charge nurse, now **that** sounds impressive. And with my friend Ruth who helped me through the rigors of nursing school and graduate training. That sounds fun.*

"5-North is an overflow unit. You'll get some med-surg, some respiratory, neuro and ortho, and some psych and alcohol cases." She stops briefly, and then adds, "Oh, and a few of the Docs do prostaglandin abortions on 5-North." She gives me a sly look to see how I am reacting to this, but I just sit, still beaming. I don't know what prostaglandin is but

I'm not asking her. And this is so exciting. A promotion!

*   *   *

I proudly announce to Kim, the nurse who has been showing us the ropes these three months, that Ruth and I are going to be working together on 5-North. Kim smiles bleakly, too bleakly for my taste, and says, "That's a rough floor. None of the staff want to go up there." I look at her nonchalantly. She adds, "Do you know that they do abortions up there?"

"Yes, of course," I retort indignantly. I know what I am getting into. *And how bad can abortions be?* There surely couldn't be that much to do except hold a woman's hand and offer reassurance. And I don't have any of those old-fashioned ideas about abortions being wrong. After all, it is 1977 and abortions have been legal for four years now. They have led us out of the dark ages. Every woman has a right to control her own body and make her own choice about reproduction.

*   *   *

As it turned out, Ruth and I didn't actually work together all that much, as we had to alternate our days off. So four evenings a week, one of us was in charge of 5-North while the other hung out at the pool at our apartment. The other working day we'd be together and alternate who was in charge that night.

Being in charge meant that we'd make the patient assignments, and take the lightest patient load so that we could stick close to the nurses' station and go on rounds with all the physicians and then brief the other staff regarding new doctor orders. 5-North was a small 14 patient unit so we only had 2 nurses and one aide on at a time.

On other floors being 'in charge' also implied that we had some authority over the other R.N.s, L.P.N.s, and nurses aides that worked the unit. In our case that wasn't true because neither Ruth nor I knew enough to tell anyone else what to do; in fact we needed help with our own jobs.

Luckily for us, we had two wonderful L.P.N.s, Lou and Minnie, who had worked the unit for a lot of years and taught us our responsibilities and supported us. They also kept track of our nurse's aides while doing their own excellent patient care. It was unfair that Ruth and I had the titles and made the "big bucks" (five dollars an hour!) while Lou and Minnie actually ran the floor. We still owe those women for their compassion towards us.

The trade-off for helping us and not making our lives miserable, as only L.P.N.s can do to new R.N.s, was that Ruth and I were expected to take care of all the abortion patients ourselves. Lou and Minnie refused to care for these patients on religious grounds and threatened to leave the floor if they were forced to help the doctor with the procedure or care for these patients in any way. This seemed fair to us.

Ruth and I had been told by our head nurse that if we had a problem with the idea of the abortion, we didn't actually *have* to assist the physician with the actual prostaglandin injection, but we did have to care for the patients afterwards.

Naturally, we thought to ourselves. It never occurred to us not to take care of the patients. And we had no trouble with the idea of assisting the doctor with the procedure; why would we not want to assist the doctor? And if we didn't, who would? Everyone knew that doctors can't do procedures alone.

*   *   *

Patricia Taylor

"In room 500 is a Susan Jones, 15 year old patient of Dr. Howard. She's a 20-weeker in for prostaglandin. Her mother brought her in and left her with her boyfriend. She's admitted, but needs an IV of normal saline. Get it in, and everything ready in the procedure room by the time Dr. Howard gets here at five. There's a list of what you need in the chart." I hear this over the tape recorder. I'm in the break room listening with Minnie, where the morning shift has taped their report for us.

Wow! I'm finally getting to take care of my first abortion patient. I'm excited because it is something new, but also a little scared because I don't know what to expect. I know Minnie won't help me, and Ruth is off. But Dr. Howard is sure to write orders, and I'll just follow those.

Surely I can be a good support person for Susan Jones. After all, I learned a lot about therapeutic communication in nursing school. I'll make sure and plan extra time to talk with her. I want to make sure that she feels good about her choice and about herself for making it. It's important that she doesn't have any guilt or regrets after this, so she can go on to live a happy life.

*   *   *

Susan Jones looks shy and quiet and very nervous sitting with sheets pulled up to her neck in her hospital bed. She is a pretty blond-haired, green-eyed beauty. Her boyfriend sits beside her holding her hand under the covers and introduces himself as Joey. He is dark-haired and has the beginnings of a mustache on his thin face. I talk to them about generalities, about things like where they go to high school, hoping they will warm up to me. They answer direct questions but do not volunteer any information.

It takes awhile for me to convince Susan to let me examine her, but finally she agrees to let me look under her covers. Joey continues to hold her hand. She is thin and her body looks like a normal teenager's body except for a definite bulge. I listen to her lungs, heart, and abdomen and then I cover her back up and then start an intravenous line with glucose and saline in her free arm. They both watch everything I do while clutching each other's hands, but neither make any comment.

The day nurse told me earlier that Susan's mother had just found out about the pregnancy. Susan hadn't told her anything, but the mother finally became suspicious when she saw Susan naked in the bathroom at home. She immediately arranged an abortion. Susan's older sister is planning on getting married next month and the mother did not want Susan to be an obviously pregnant bridesmaid.

I try to talk to them again after the exam. Susan doesn't offer any information. I ask open questions; "What is this like for you?" But she won't answer, except to say "I don't know," and I can't tell what she is feeling. Her facial expressions just show fear. Joey's expressions seem sadder but he won't talk either. I start to doubt my ability to communicate therapeutically and I feel frustration with them for not responding to my efforts.

When I tell them that Susan will need to go to another room without Joey for the procedure, tears start to well up in Susan's eyes and Joey holds her hand more tightly with both of his, and I suddenly feel very sorry for them.

I explain that the doctor will clean Susan's abdomen and then numb an area so that he can inject a medication called Prostaglandin through her skin into her uterus that will start premature labor. Ideally, I would tell them a lot more about what to expect, but I really don't know myself.

When Dr. Howard comes to the unit, I walk Susan down the hall to the exam room, and leave Joey sitting, quiet and pale in the corner.

I help her to sit up on the table, and then to lie flat on her back. Susan looks younger and more defeated than she did with Joey by her side. She passively lets me position her as I choose. She is wearing just a faded yellow hospital gown that hangs over the edge of the narrow table. I cover her from the waist down with a sheet, put a pillow under her head, adjust her I.V. fluids, pour the disinfectant, Betadine, into a sterile bowl, pull up the lidocaine in a syringe, and then open sterile gauze pads next to all the supplies I have already assembled. Susan quietly stares at the ceiling with her arms lying limply at her sides. I want to say something comforting but can't think of anything to say, so am quiet too.

Dr. Howard joins us--a large, dark, unsmiling man in a stained lab coat that he hangs on a chair. He says, "Hello" nodding at Susan and, "Has the permit been signed?" glaring at me. Susan nods hopelessly as I reply, "Susan's mother signed them before she left." I hold Susan's hand and tell her that it will be O.K. that it will be over soon, that all she has to do is relax-- those ubiquitous nursing phrases.

The doctor puts on sterile gloves and dips the gauze in the Betadine while I uncover Susan's protruding abdomen. She winces as he rubs the cold, brown- red solution over a large area of her skin, and I push the hair back from her forehead and say, "It is just cold."

After several more washings, Dr. Howard, with the words "This will sting a little," injects a syringe of lidocaine into Susan's 'belly button' on her taunt abdomen. She tenses and gasps.

He picks up a large pre-filled syringe labeled *Prostaglandin* with a very long needle, tells Susan "hold still," and plunges the thick needle and then the solution into what is presumably the amniotic sac through the umbilicus. There couldn't possibly have been time for the area to have become numbed by the lidocaine.

Susan cries out and I instruct her to "take some deep breaths." I feel a little queasy, and take a deep breath myself. She starts to sob and I want to too.

"Now we just have to wait and let it take its course. You might be uncomfortable but we can't give you anything that might slow things down," Dr. Howard says as he puts back on his coat and leaves the room.

*　　*　　*

"Well, the worst is over now," I tell Susan and Joey as I help Susan back into her bed. She has stopped crying and is quiet while I tell Joey what has happened and what the doctor said about just having to wait. I suggest that they watch T.V. as I remember learning that distraction does wonders at times like these.

I return to the exam room to clean up and then rush to check on my other patients, who I've been neglecting all this time. I wish Ruth were on tonight as it is busy and I feel overwhelmed. As usual though, Minnie is holding me above water. She asks me about Susan and I tell her Susan is doing 'O.K.'

"I'll be praying for that girl."

*　　*　　*

I'm trying to check off some doctor's orders when Susan's call light comes on. I ask the nurses' aide to check on Susan but she returns to tell me that Susan wants *me*. I sigh and leave my paperwork to head down the long hall; Susan's room is the last on the right which is reserved I'm told for "the abortions, because the sicker patients need to be closer to the nurses' station."

When I enter her room it is dark and both Susan and Joey are in the bathroom, with the only light. She is sitting on the toilet, grabbing her swollen abdomen, rocking back and forth, and crying. Joey is kneeling

　　　Patricia Taylor

on the floor holding the garbage can under her chin, looking as if he is about to cry. She has obviously been vomiting and having diarrhea at the same time. Her I.V. line is stretched out behind Joey from the pole in the doorway, and blood is backing up into the line.

I wedge into the bathroom with them and pull the I.V. pole closer and turn up the fluid to try to flush the line. I pull a washcloth off the rack, wet it under the faucet, and wipe Susan's face and mouth. "I'll see if I can get you anything, but you need to get back in bed," I implore. But Susan refuses to move.

In the nurses' station, I call the nursing supervisor on the phone to ask if I can call the doctor about Susan. It is a house rule that I have to call the supervisor before the doctor. The rule was formed to prevent new graduates from calling the doctor about something that is not really important. Of course, it is almost always something important to the patient, but that is just a minor technicality. We aren't given permission to call very often.

And the supervisor says that I most definitely am not to call Dr. Howard about Susan. "His abortions are always like this. Any medication now will stop contractions and we want her to labor. That's just how it is."

"O.K.," I mutter.

"Oh, and Annie on 11-7 just called in. Will you work a double?" she asks innocently, a supervisor's favorite question.

"Sure," I reply thinking only about the new car I'm saving for.

As I'm walking back to Susan's room, it hits me that I've committed myself to another eight hours and I don't have a clue how to help Susan. She and Joey are in the exact positions I left them in. I tell her we will just have to make her as comfortable as possible as I can't give her anything for the pain. She cries as Joey helps me convince her to get back in bed. We change her soiled gown and position her on her side. I show Joey how to rub her lower back.

When she calms down some, I tell them both to try to relax and I leave them with the lights turned down in the room and with the nursing call bell in reach.

This is ridiculous, I think walking back to the desk. I remember what it was like for women in labor when we did our O.B. rotation in school. They were in labor; they couldn't relax! I just hadn't realized that Susan would have to labor. For an abortion? It just didn't fit.

*   *   *

The night is dragging; I'm staring at the institutional green walls and barely able to keep my eyes open. It took me hours to get everyone settled down; everyone, it seemed, needed sleeping or pain medicine. Everyone is resting now—except Susan of course. She has been back and forth to the bathroom all night. I keep checking on them but there is not much I can do.

When I think that Susan is close to delivering the "birth contents" I am supposed to call the O.B. unit so they can take her over to their floor for the delivery. So I keep looking for blood or other fluid that would indicate signs of a delivery whenever I check on her, but I don't see any.

Joey is with her all the time. What do people do who are alone? Surely not everyone has someone like Joey to be there like this.

*   *   *

It is close to dawn as I try to finish my paperwork, and I hear Susan yelling loudly from the other end of the hall. I think to call the O.B. Department, but decide to wait and check her myself first.

Patricia Taylor

She is in bed with the head of the bed up, naked, with the sheet up to her waist, writhing and screaming. Joey is in bed with her trying to soothe her. She cries out, "I can't stand this anymore. I'm going to die!" She looks pale and her hair is wet with perspiration. Joey looks totally frazzled. I put on gloves and wonder how much longer this will take.

Suddenly she yells out even louder than before and then becomes still, staring with wide eyes. Then, just as suddenly, she pulls back the sheet and leans forward to look between her legs. She inhales noisily, and Joey and I look where she is looking. Her thighs and the sheet between her legs are covered with blood.

And there is a baby! A perfectly formed little girl who we can see under layers of blood and other fluids. She is about a foot long and her cord is still hanging from Susan. The baby has clear gelatinous skin, tiny closed eyelids, and perfect little hands and feet that don't move at all. But her mouth is open and it is gasping for air; the little rib cages are sucking in and out.

I try to pull the sheet back over the baby but Joey grabs the sheet from me, and we all three stare at the baby in uncomprehending amazement and horror.

Finally I grab the nurses' call light and when the night L.P.N. answers, I tell her to call O.B. I dry off the infant's head and wrap the tiny body and in a towel and let Susan hold her, which she begs to do.

*   *   *

The baby quit breathing before Ellen, the O.B. nurse got there. Ellen delivered the placenta, instructed me how to take care of Susan post-partum, and carried the baby and the placenta to the hospital lab.

Susan and Joey aren't saying anything; she occasionally starts to cry and then stops. Joey still quietly sits by her side, still holding her hand. I mechanically clean Susan up and make sure she doesn't have too much bleeding after the procedure.

I report what happened with Susan and the baby to the day shift, and they tell me that the infant must have been twenty-four to twenty-six weeks old. "That happens sometimes with Dr. Howard's patients." The head nurse says that it is illegal to do an abortion past 20 weeks, but "Dr. Howard often incorrectly estimates the dates."

Like on purpose?

I wonder about this, but don't say anything. The nurses seem sad but have that hopeless attitude like they've seen this happen before and probably will again.

*   *   *

Susan will go home today. And I assume Joey will continue to be there for her. I guess she'll recuperate to be a bridesmaid in her sister's wedding. And no doubt she and her mother will look pretty in the proud family pictures. Ruth will plunge in for another day on the job as the charge nurse. And I, I have a whole day off to sleep in the sun and dream about the car I'm going to buy with my new promotion.

Zero to Ten

"*M*ars admitting Neck, twelve hundred, 303, dressings needed ASAP!" Susan yells to me as I whiz by the nurses' station with an IV pole, a bed pan, a clipboard, and a stethoscope around my neck. My pockets over-flow with gloves, scissors, pens, tape, hemostat, needles, alcohol pads, small gauze pads, adhesive remover, lip gloss and breath mints. "Wonderful, my character is improving by the minute!" I pronounce as I run past the nursing station into the medicine room to fill a syringe with medication. We just discussed yesterday how challenges and crises could improve our character. On this cancer floor we seem to have more than our share of opportunities for improvement.

"Neck, 303, Mars admitting. Do ya hear me?" Susan yells again from behind the nursing station desk. She is our ward clerk and she keeps tabs on whose turn it is to take the next admission. Her communication skills are somewhat lacking but I understand from months of working with this hospital lingo that Dr. Mars, one of our cancer doctors, is admitting a patient with some type of neck cancer and an open wound at around noon. Hence the need to have dressing supplies in room 303 as soon as possible so that when the doctor comes to see the patient he will not have to wait on them. There is an unspoken rule in this place that everyone's major priority is not to inconvenience the doctors, even if it means severely inconveniencing a patient.

"Yes, how could I not hear you?" I yell back as I charge down the hall that is full of sick, anxious patients waiting for me to make them feel better. The I.V. pole squeaks, sticks, and goes in the wrong direction like those jitneys in the grocery store. The hall is long. Whoever designed this unit couldn't have been a nurse, and probably wasn't real clear on reality either. Every trip to and from a patient's room is like a marathon. At least I don't have to jog when I get home. My Disney World Goofy watch says that it is now 11 am. I have an hour to get caught up. Shouldn't be too hard as long as I don't plan on having any lunch or drink breaks. Or for that matter, I shouldn't plan any bathroom trips for the rest of the day either.

I leave the IV pole in the hall outside of room 300 and enter with a bedpan and a clipboard. Mrs. Walker is lying in bed partly on her left side in an awkward position with a large triangle-shaped pillow strapped between her legs: the pillow is supposed to keep her hip joint in proper position after her surgery. Her right leg sticks out from under the covers. She is an elderly appearing woman with no hair because of recent chemotherapy; she is dressed in a dull blue hospital gown that is slipping from her shoulders and a purple turban that is slipping off her head. She recently broke a hip because her bones are so weak from bone cancer, and she's been in a great deal of pain. Mrs. Walker is understandably very unhappy about her situation, and she makes sure that everyone comprehends this fact.

I go into the bathroom and wash my hands while I tell her that I have her pain injection and a new bedpan for her. She says, "It's about time." The last pan was too large and caused her a great deal of pain to maneuver onto. I ask her what her pain is on a scale of zero to ten if ten is the worst ever, and she says it is a fifteen. I put on a pair of my gloves, powder the bedpan, and pull down her side rail. I clean a spot on her left hip with alcohol, inject her muscle with a narcotic and then position the bed-pan under her. I make sure she can reach her call button, I pull the side rail up, and I tell her to call me as soon as she is finished.

"Don't be too long," she moans as I go back to the bathroom, remove my gloves and wash my hands.

Patricia Taylor

I've learned to wash my hands before and after caring for every patient. It's one of the few things I remember from nursing school, probably because it's the first thing we learned. We even lined up in front of a sink and washed our hands one by one as our instructor watched. Since I've worked with cancer patients I've come to realize that most people with cancer die from infections, not the cancer itself. And a lot of those infections come from us as we carry bugs from room to room. This is before we find out about the HIV virus and wearing gloves to protect ourselves too.

So with my clean hands and clipboard in tow, I grab the IV pole and scuttle to the next room. I'm thinking that I must get those dressings ready for Dr. Mars, but first I need to check on the guy in 305.

Mr. Henry is a young good-looking man in his early 30's who has just completed his first chemotherapy treatment. He's pale, and his muddy brown hair sticks up from his head. He's wearing plaid men's pajamas like my grandfather used to wear. He has been waiting for a rolling IV pole so that he can go to the bathroom instead of using the urinal. I walk in, say I'm sorry for keeping him waiting, disconnect the clear intravenous fluid from the pole attached to the bed, hang it on the wobbly pole I have brought for him, and check his intravenous site for any signs of problems. He looks up at me and smiles: a bleak, brave smile. I help him to sit on the side of the bed and then to walk to the bathroom while I push the pole ahead of us.

I shut the bathroom door and then stand on the other side of it while I listen for any signs of distress, check my clipboard for things I need to do, and watch the picture on the T.V. set. Donahue is interviewing some women and men on stage who do not have any clothes on from the waist up and I wonder what they are saying. Mr. Henry seems to be taking a long time and I yell out to ask him if he is all right.

"Get me back to bed," he finally calls out. I help him pull up his brown plaid P.J. bottoms and walk back to the bed, while pushing the pole again. He is paler than before and is perspiring. He states he is having diarrhea and is nauseated. I help him to lie down in bed with his head up and on his side and then get a wet cold washcloth to put on his forehead, and a towel and a pan to put near his head. He mumbles, "This damn cancer!" I tell him I agree, and stand looking sorrowfully at him a few minutes, with my hand on his. The frequent feeling of powerlessness overcomes me for a few minutes, and then I get back to my busy mode to do what little I can.

"I'll get you some medication," I say, as if that is the answer to everything. I don gloves, measure the amount and then empty the pans in the toilet that collected the liquid stool and his urine. We call these pans "pilgrim's hats" because when they are turned upside down they resemble those hats that pilgrims wore in pictures in textbooks. They have a rounded bowl the size of a head in the center and a wide brim around the edge. The similarity ends there, however, as they are white plastic and have measuring lines and numbers on the inside. Two can be placed in the toilet facing each other and stool and urine can be collected at the same time. It's amazing what modern science has achieved.

I wash my hands and then record the time and the amount of stool and urine, and Mr. Henry's complaints of diarrhea and nausea on my clipboard. On this board I have written every piece of information regarding every patient for the entire day. Without my "cheat sheet" I am hopelessly lost.

I practically run back to the nurses' station to get medication for Mr. Henry and to record the injection I gave Mrs. Walker. I notice that her light over her door has not come on yet, which would be the signal for me that she was ready to get off the bedpan. I am relieved that I have a few more minutes.

When I get to the medication cart I have to wait for another nurse to use it, so I go looking for the nurse who happens to have the keys to the narcotic cabinet at that moment. There's only one set of these keys for the entire unit and there are five registered nurses who need them regularly. Whoever thought of this idea should be shot. Surely if we can be trusted to make life-and-death decisions on a daily basis we can be trusted to carry a set of keys all day long and keep our paws off the drugs!

Susan screams at me again, "Better get that stuff ready for Dr. Mars. Her neck patient will be here at noon."

"I know. I know," I say with gritted teeth as I proceed to get the keys from another nurse who was at the end of the hall, and then the medicine I need for Mr. Henry. As I am going back to him I notice that Mrs. Walker's light is on over her door now, and I yell to her that I will be right there. When I get to Mr. Henry, I see that he has vomited into his pan and he looks more green now than pale, the same color as his vomit. I wash my hands and then slowly administer medication into his IV line while I assure him that this will help, but that he must not try to get up out of bed alone. He says, "No problem." I empty and measure and throw away the vomit and refresh the cool cloth to his head. Then I give him some anti-diarrhea medicine with a sip of water and wash my hands.

I pull up the side-rail and tell him to call me if he needs me and I will be back to check on him as soon as possible. This is my usual line when leaving a patient who is very sick and about whom I feel guilty for leaving. I make a note on my clipboard to record his medication later along with the new amount of emesis, and eyeball his IV one more time. He will need another bag of fluid soon.

When I get to Mrs. Walker's room she is very unhappy with me and tells me that her pain is worse than before because she has had to sit on the bedpan so long. I apologize and tell her that I know she is very uncomfortable and unhappy. "You bet I am," she rejoins. I wash my hands and put on gloves, pull down the side rail, turn her again, remove the pan, wipe and clean her perineal area with water and soap, measure, empty, and rinse the pan, assist her to turn to her right side, pull her gown up and tie it around her neck and straighten her turban. To ease her pain and to help her rest, and to assuage my feelings of inadequacy, I rub her back for awhile and talk to her soothingly. I use that smelly, ineffective hospital lotion and wish I had some Avon Moisture Therapy Lotion for her. It wouldn't hurt *my* hands any either, as they are raw from so much hand washing.

I ask her how her pain is now on a scale of zero to ten, and she says it is still a fifteen. I pull up her side rail and tell her that maybe she can rest a little, and that she should call me if she needs me, and that I will be back as soon as possible. I give her a sip of cool water and remind her to drink a lot of fluids. She says she will if someone offers them to her. I wish fervently that a family member would come and sit with her. I wash my hands and record everything on my clipboard including a note to call her daughter and suggest that someone stay with her mother.

As I head back to the nurses' station to collect those darn dressing supplies for Dr. Mars, I see Mrs. Jones outside of room 304. She is the wife of Mr. Jones who is supposed to be discharged today as soon as I finish his paperwork. She is sighing heavily and looking pointedly at her watch. I detour back toward her and apologize for holding them up. That seems to be my major form of communication these days.

Mr. Jones is sitting in a chair by his bed and he is fully clothed in black pants, a forest green pull-over sweater and black loafers. He looks frail, but pleased to be going home. His wife has apparently packed his belongings as he is surrounded by a suitcase and several full plastic bags printed with the hospital logo. The bedside table holds plants and flower arrangements. She is pacing the room when I enter. I wash my hands and then perch on the end of his bed, which I'm not supposed to do because of germs and because it is the patient's personal property. But my feet need a break and he doesn't seem to care, as he is not accepting anything around here as his own. I do what is called discharge teaching, which means I tell them about how to take care of Mr. Jones when they go home.

He has recently been diagnosed with colon cancer and has just started his first radiation therapy. I review what medications he needs to take as well as side effects of each and what to report to his physician. I tell him not to wash the area of his skin that is within his tattoos with soap as it might cause skin irritation. Tattoos are permanent marks the size of the top of a straight pin that have been placed on his abdomen to direct the therapist to aim the radiation at exactly the same place each treatment. I also suggest that he eat lots of bananas, cheese, marshmallows, pretzels and milkshakes as he might have trouble with diarrhea and a loss of appetite. I tell them that he will not have to worry about his hair falling out as only his bowels will be affected by the radiation, and that he might be more tired than usual so take it easy. He states that he does not expect to have any problems and that he is ready to go. I have him sign and then give him a carbon copy of his teaching sheet, and then charge down the hall to find a wheelchair and a rolling cart for all his belongings.

"303 in admitting! Mars will be here soon!" yells Susan.

"O.K.," I say deliberately, trying to sound calm and in control. It is almost as if she is enjoying watching me suffer but I know that she is trying to help me to get my priorities straight and have those dressings ready for the great Doctor. When I go by the nursing station, she yells out a list of the dressing supplies I am supposed to be collecting, and I stop long enough to write them down on my clipboard..

I practically fly back to room 304 with the wheelchair. I mean, the wheels are burning rubber. Mr. Jones gets in the chair after an explanation that it is hospital policy for him to go downstairs in a wheelchair and then Mrs. Jones and I pile most of his belonging onto the cart, and the rest on his lap, including a large flowering plant. I wheel him down the hall, and then into an elevator, with Mrs. Jones following with the cart.

At the front door of the hospital I wait with Mr. Jones while his wife goes to get their car. He tells me about their five pit bulls and how he is anxious to get home to them. He says that they sleep with him and his wife in a king-size bed. As I load him and his belongings into the car, I think to myself that it certainly does take all kinds.

When I get back on the unit, Susan tells me that Dr. Love is on the phone about Mr. Little's bloodwork results. I think to myself, *Bloodwork? What bloodwork? Did Mr. Little have bloodwork? Have I seen Mr. Little since I assessed him this morning? Is Mr. Little still alive? Where is my clipboard?*

*   *   *

A "pink lady" in a pink smock with pink hair wheels my new patient toward room 303 and on the way introduces the patient to me as Mrs. Lott. My first thought is about the dressings and how mad Dr. Mars is going to be if they are not in the room when she gets here; then I appropriately refocus and tell Mrs. Lott that I will be her nurse until 3 pm. It's like being someone's waitress for the next few hours but I can offer more complex services. I don't tell Mrs. Lott this. I smile and accompany her to her room, wash my hands, then assist her to sit on the bed. She states she wants to sit up until her husband comes with her nightgown.

She is a very attractive woman in her late 50's, the type of person who looks like they would never adjust well to aging. Her auburn hair is pulled back in a neat bun, and she has on a complete face of makeup including a modest cinnamon lipstick. She has on a beige turtleneck with a very high collar and a green vest with elephants on it, and large elephant-shaped earrings. I notice that there is a piece of gauze extending out of the right side of the outfit and that the shirt and vest are bulging on that side. I also smell an offensive odor over the wafting of Channel #5 perfume, but I keep that assessment to myself. It is the smell I am so familiar with since working with these patients; it is a unique smell of cancer and occurs with tumors that have not been treated or have been treated but the cancer has won the battle. I orient her to her room and explain how all the buttons on the bed work. I tell her to be comfortable and I will be right back and then I charge back down the hall to the nurses' station again.

On the way, I peek my head in all my patient's rooms. Mr. Little appears to be alive and sleeping. Thank God. Mr. Henry looks happy with his girlfriend lying in his bed with him and a definite odor of marijuana surrounding them. Thank God. I close the door tightly and put a "Do Not Disturb" sign on it. Mrs. Walker doesn't complain to me at all as she is now complaining to her pastor who is sitting at the bedside looking pained and patient. Thank God.

I grab an admission kit for Mrs. Lott that contains a water pitcher, a cup, an emesis basin, some Kleenex and that wonderful hospital lotion. Also I collect all the dressing supplies that Dr. Mars ordered ASAP hours ago. Luckily I can count on no one being on time around here. Unfortunately, that applies to me too. I just finished my 12:00 meds at 1:30. I make sure and charge the patient for every item I take, as this is also a major priority in this hospital, and every hospital for that matter.

When I get back to Mrs. Lott's room, I put down all the supplies and then I wash my hands. I take the admission form that I collected earlier off my clipboard and explain to Mrs. Lott that I need to ask some questions and look and listen to her body for an initial assessment. She states she is not comfortable with the looking part so I start by asking questions about her physical complaints, her personal life, and her concerns, so that later I can write up a nursing care plan for her. I am as therapeutic as I know how to be considering I'm very rushed.

She does end up opening up to me, which is good because she originally wasn't too thrilled about the question and answer part either. She says that she has had a sore on her neck for several months and that it is getting bigger. She did not go to a doctor because she doesn't like them (Who does?) but that she finally went to her personal physician yesterday because the sore is starting to bleed and she has not been able to stop it. She was referred to Dr. Mars, who insisted that Mrs. Lott come into the hospital today. Mrs. Lott hopes to be treated quickly with "antibiotics or something" so that she can go home.

Mrs. Lott's husband arrives with a large suitcase full of her personal things. He appears much older than his wife and immediately starts to unpack everything and to ask her where she wants them. He is quiet other than that, and only responds with a nod when I introduce myself. I leave the room to check on my other patients one more time, and to give the next shift report on tape while Mrs. Lott changes into her own nightgown. I told her she was supposed to wear the supplied hospital gown but wasn't going to fight her about that.

At 2:30 I go back to Mrs. Lott's room, wash my hands, check her vital signs, look over her body, and listen to her lungs, heart, and bowels. I now see a large dressing on her neck that has old blood on most of it. She keeps this covered with a towel and a green bed jacket that looks just great with her red hair. As I am finishing up, Dr. Mars enters the room.

Mars nods to Mrs. Lott and says "How are you?" and then immediately, without waiting for an answer, goes to the bed and pulls back the bed jacket and the towel. He complains that it is difficult to get to the wound because of the personal nightgown so I have to help Mrs. Lott pull it over her head and the bulky dressing. Then Mars instructs me to begin opening packages so that he can change the dressing, and he puts on gloves and begins to remove the old one. Under the dressing is a large ulcerated wound over the entire right side of the neck that is continually trickling a small amount of blood. The smell that I noticed earlier is much more pronounced now. *Note to self: bring some incense tomorrow.* That is the only thing that will cut this odor.

As Dr. Mars changes the dressing he mentions that the tumor is close to the Carotid artery. Neither Mrs. or Mr. Lott seem to realize the significance of this, and do not ask any questions. When the new dressing is in place, Dr. Mars instructs me to change it "P.R.N." which means whenever it is needed and tells his patient that a radiation therapy doctor will be in later in the day. Mrs. Lott tells the doctor that she doesn't want any radiation, but Dr. Mars says, "You have to or you are going to die," and then leaves the room.

Mrs. Lott starts to cry and holds the sheet up to her neck to cover her naked chest. I sit on one side of the bed and hold her hand while her husband sits on the other side of the bed and looks at her imploringly. When she stops crying, I help her put her nightgown back on, and I tell her that she has a right to make her own decisions. I also try to tell them in a gentle way that this really is serious, but they don't seem to believe me and keep saying they just want to go home. Finally, I say that another nurse will be in to take care of her tonight. I tell them both that I will be back at 7:00 in the morning and that I will be thinking of them. A lot of help that will be!

*   *   *

At 3:15 I finally start working on Mrs. Lott's care plan, which will show all the nurses how to give her special, holistic, individualized care.

After this, I plan to chart on all the patient's records about everything that has happened today. I'm supposed to be going home in 15 minutes but will have to explain to my supervisor again why I need overtime. I'm hungry, thirsty, tired; my feet are aching; and I really need to go to the bathroom; so when the nursing call light comes on beeping for room 303 I ignore it by justifying that the next shift will be getting out of report any minute. But, after 5 minutes, the light is still beeping and no one else has volunteered to get it, so I get up and trudge down the hall.

When I enter room 303, Mrs. Lott is clutching the towel to her neck and the bed jacket has gone askew. She looks frightened and when I get closer I notice the dressing has loosened and is saturated with bright red blood that is oozing much more quickly now and is running down her chest. Mr. Lott is sitting next to her looking concerned but not really afraid.

I yell at them, "Why didn't you use the emergency light in the bathroom?" and immediately recognize my non-therapeutic question as a response to my own guilt for not coming sooner.

"I didn't want to bother you," she says. I grab some towels from the bathroom and pull the emergency cord, then press the towels against her neck. I try very hard to look professional and in control while I think about Dr. Mars's words, **close to the carotid artery,** and wonder what I am going to do. Another nurse, Bob, runs in and I ask him to get the code cart and to call Dr. Mars. I tell Mrs. Lott to hold the towels as I unwrap the stethoscope from around my neck and pull the cuff from the wall to get her blood pressure.

Suddenly she lurches forward, drops the towels, and gasps.

Patricia Taylor

Blood is spurting from her neck now and the dressing is falling off. I drop the cuff, pick up the extra towels, gather up what I can of the sheets, and press them against her neck. I get up on the bed with her, on my knees, straddling her, to give me more leverage. Blood is covering my hands and my Goofy watch. I realize I didn't wash my hands or put on gloves and that it is too late now.

Her eyes are bulging and she is trying to fight me off. She is gasping for breath and looking panicked. I know she knows she is dying. I put my arms around her. The towels and sheet are dripping with blood and are slipping off her. Blood is spurting over the bed, the walls, the ceiling, and me. Slowly she starts to slump back on to the bed and I go down with her. When she stops moving, I feel for a carotid pulse on the left side of her neck and it is very faint. Soon the pulse stops and she lies very still with her eyes and mouth gaping.

Bob runs into the room and tells me that Dr. Mars has ordered a "No Code." I think, *Good*, because I'm not about to do one now anyway. That would have meant pounding on her chest and sticking a tube down her throat, which, obviously, would be ridiculous.

Suddenly, I remember Mr. Lott. He is sitting in the chair next to the bed looking at us without much expression on his face. I get up and pull the covers up to Mrs. Lott's neck and straighten her head. I dab at the blood on her face with a towel that had fallen on another nearby chair.

Then I look at him and say "She's gone." He ignores me and stands up over to his wife. I notice he has blood on his white shirt and face. He says to her, "Come on now honey. Wake up."

"I'll stay with you awhile," I volunteer.

"No, you go on, we'll be all right."

*   *   *

In the bathroom I take off my blood soaked uniform and put it in the garbage. It was my brand new one with the cute pink jumper and extra large pockets. I wash my shoes, arms, hands, watch, hair and face and then put on a torn hospital green scrub suit that someone brought me from surgery. I'm stunned and feel nauseated like I always do when I witness an unfair, unexpected death. I can't cry though I'd wish I could. I feel unbearable sadness for Mr. Lott, who finally had to be taken away by his son and daughter-in-law.

Yet I also feel honored to have been the one holding Mrs. Lott when she died. Sharing her death was such an intimate moment; more powerful but similar to the experience I've had on Good Friday when I washed other's feet. I walk slowly back down the long hall one more time today to clean and prepare her body for the funeral home. I wash my hands and put on gloves.

Patricia Taylor

Sex On The Beach

"*H*ave you had a drink called Sex on the Beach?" Cheryl asked me as we rolled Dave towards her so I could rub his back with coconut lotion. She'd just gotten back from vacation on St. Simon's island and was talking about her experiences there. We were leaning over either side of Dave's hospital bed and finishing up his bath. He hadn't said a word in several days and we'd forgotten the rule to assume your patient can hear you even when he isn't speaking.

"Sex on the beach? When did we have sex on the beach?" Dave piped up. Cheryl and I laughed.

"Dave, Sex on the beach is the name of a drink. It's like a tequila sunrise. Have you ever had one?" I asked, happy to have him talking to us again. Hope rose in me that this was somehow a sign of recovery. But it wasn't to be.

"When did we have sex on the beach?" was his only reply.

*   *   *

Dave had been admitted to our cancer floor with complications of the AIDS virus six weeks before that discussion. He was among a number of young men admitted with the same diagnosis over the last couple of years since the virus had been identified. We saw more of our share of the disease than a lot of cancer units around the country because our hospital was located downtown in a large metropolitan area with a very high gay population.

And we saw a lot of deaths, as this was before there were

drugs that enable people to live with AIDS as they do with any chronic illness. Then patients reported to us that their entire social structure was dying of AIDS: most of their friends and neighbors were vanishing in a very short time period. Even our head nurse at the time, who was gay, had lost his lover and then his own life within a year.

When I first met Dave I was impressed with his demeanor. He didn't look sick, but like he was just there to visit someone. His clothes were casual but expensive and he carried a brief case. He was well built and had dark wavy hair neatly cut around his neck line. His chocolate eyes bore into me like he was really seeing me, and he had one of those smiles that made me want to tell him everything. I found out why right away: Dave's admission papers said he was a psychiatrist. I introduced myself and led him to his single room. With his soft musical southern accent he told me to call him Dave. I said "Sure" and wondered if I could marry him too. I told him to get settled and I would be back to formally admit him soon.

When I came back and started my admission questionnaire I decided to try to get to know him a little before starting on all the routine questions. I was sitting on a chair that I had pulled up at an angle by the right side of his bed, and held a clip-board with papers and pen on my lap. He was leaning up against several pillows, and his long muscular legs stretched out over the still-made hospital bed. He had all of his clothes on as if he wasn't planning on staying long. Papers were scattered over the bed-side table that was pulled near him on the other side of the bed.

I looked down at my admission form and read the basic information that Dave had already given the admission clerk. His name was David William Faulkner. "I like the ring to that, and it sounds familiar." I winked at him. "And I see that you are a doctor. Are you new around here, or just new to me?" I certainly wasn't an expert on physicians in the area, much less psychiatrists, but I'd never heard of him before, and I thought I would have remembered that name.

"Yes, as far as my life goes. I finished my residency in general psychiatry at Penn State last year and I just moved back South and am establishing my own clinic. I have an office over on Bay street. I'm getting a lot of referrals so I'm hopeful that it will go well." He gazed toward the window which happened to face that street, though we were eight blocks above it. He looked like he would fly over there if he could.

I started to warm up to him and relaxed. "I kinda thought with a name like William Faulkner, and your accent, that you must be from somewhere around here."

"Yeah, I was raised here, but I don't have any family here anymore. Both of my parents are dead and my sister is out west. But it still feels like home."

Instead of picking up on that fact that he had no close family, which would have been the helpful thing to do, I just blurted out, "Well, now I know who to call when I start having problems coping, not that I ever do." We both laughed at that. I could really be a card.

"Anyway, now I need to ask some nurse-type questions. Do you mind?" This was my standard way of starting to ask those questions that could be embarrassing but were necessary to get the whole clinical picture. (Questions like: *How often do you urinate?*; *Is your sex life satisfactory?*; *What financial concerns do you have?*; *Have you passed gas through your rectum today?*; *Are you spiritually content?*)

"Go ahead."

"What brought you here today?"

"I've been having some problems breathing when I exert myself and so I'm going to be evaluated for pneumonia. I'm probably

run down as I've been so busy moving and starting a new practice."
He said this casually like he really didn't think this would be a problem
for him; then he looked longingly at his paper work. I got the hint, but
forged ahead anyway.

"Any other symptoms?"

"No that's it. I just need a few days of antibiotics and some
rest, and then I need to get out of here because I don't have anyone
to fill in for me right now. I called my patients and canceled till next
week."

I forced a smile and said something inane about caring for
yourself before you could care for others, as if I, as a cancer nurse,
knew anything about that. I mean, does any cancer nurse? I think we
do this because we have such a need to be needed.

I continued my initial interview cheerfully like I believed that
Dave just needed a few days' rest, but I thought about how difficult
this was going to be. Dave's admission paper work stated that he
had 'Rule-out Pneumocystis carinii' which is a type of pneumonia
common to people with the AIDS virus. "Rule out" meant that they
were going to do some tests to see for sure what he had. But Dave
must have been told about this possible diagnosis by his physician,
who had a reputation for being very direct and for caring for people
with AIDS.

Dave apparently was choosing not to deal with it then. And I at
least knew enough not to push the information on him. I played along
with his fantasy that he would be better and back to life as normal
soon. We learned in nursing school that it was important not to try to
push people out of their denial. They needed it for a reason.

Walking back to the nurses' station I wondered if Dave
was gay. Most of the men we saw with AIDS were gay back then,
especially the single ones like Dave. But he didn't seem like most of

the men who came in with a designated male lover and a multitude of male friends to offer support.

It was a few days later when I noticed that Dave didn't have visitors at all. He said that he hadn't had time to keep up with a lot of friends over the last few years. But I thought it strange that no one came in with him when he was admitted and no one came in to visit later either, although he did talk on the phone from time to time. That happened mostly at night when I wasn't there, according to the night nurses. I thought that if he wasn't gay he would surely have a girlfriend, but that didn't seem to be the case either.

Because Dave didn't have visitors I spent a lot of time with him. I was assigned as his primary nurse which meant that I always took care of him when I was on duty, and I also started to stay after work occasionally. It wasn't a sexual thing, honestly; it was just that I felt safe somehow and better about myself when I was with him. I brought him little gifts like candy and nice-smelling lotions because he didn't get those things from anyone else.

We found out that we had a lot in common. We played the piano, enjoyed symphonies and ballet, and read classical literature. I loaned him novels, and on his good days we would discuss them.

I also brought him a book on "wellness." The author wrote about how to improve your immune system with nutrition, positive thinking, meditation, and visualization of the good cells multiplying and fighting any bad cells. Dave read it in bits and pieces; I could see that the book mark was slowly moving to the back of the book. He didn't talk about it though.

He did have Pneumocystis carinii and had gotten very sick with it. And then, when he partially recovered from that, he developed purple sores on his legs that were also related to the AIDS virus; he was diagnosed with Kaposi's Sarcoma. He still talked about getting out soon, and not at all about the seriousness of his diagnoses or his prognosis. It was as if he'd never heard the word AIDS.

* * *

On one of Dave's good days, he asked me to wheel him in a chair up to the roof. The "roof" was really a screened-in area on the tenth and top floor of the hospital which was open to patients and visitors. He used to walk up there by himself every day during the first week when he was still feeling pretty well. Our unit census was low, so I had the luxury to take him up. Slow days were very rare and considered a real blessing because you could actually have quality time with your patients, which was the reason most of us went into nursing in the first place.

Dave and I could see the city from there which stretched for miles. The sky was clear and cool, and the auburn colors of fall were everywhere. It was quiet, too, compared to the usual hustle, because the day was a Sunday and most people had stayed in the suburbs. There were some children playing in the screened in area. They were laughing happily. Dave sat in his wheelchair and looked at the scenery for a long time. I sat beside him on a plastic chair, took a deep breath, and let myself relax a little bit from the usual constant hectic pace.

Finally, he spoke. "How could anyone see a day like today and not believe that there is a God?"

Well, it wasn't too hard for me. Usually on a day like that I was running from room to room filled with people who were sick and dying. "I'm not sure . . .," I started, while looking down.

Dave turned his now-familiar dark eyes on me. "I have to believe that there is a God who cares. Otherwise what is the point?"

I faced him and wondered if he was thinking about his own

Patricia Taylor

life and imminent death. "I'm not sure that I can believe there is a reason for all of this, but I'd like to," I replied.

Dave looked back out over the city. "St. Augustine said that if we take a leap toward faith that God will illuminate the soul and give us a knowledge of his existence. And he said that 1300 years before Kierkegaard was conceived."

My eyes widened. I didn't realize that Dave was *that* deep.

"That's why my practice is so important to me. I think that God wants me to love people and try to help them find some quality of life for themselves. And it seems like the least I can do for a God who created me and loves me."

Never at a loss for words, I tried an answer: "Well I believe that it's important to help people too. I'm not happy unless I think I'm really working hard and making a difference in people's lives. I'm just not sure about the God part."

He smiled at me, and I said that I should probably get back down stairs. We never had that discussion again, but I thought about it.

*   *   *

Dave had lost a lot of weight and had no interest in trying to drink milkshakes, which is the nurse's answer to all appetite problems. (This is probably because we wish so badly someone would tell us that *we* had to drink several chocolate milkshakes a day.) He was spending almost all of his time in bed. With an occasional burst of new energy he'd make it to the chair with help. He'd spent a lot of time reading case files until he finally was forced to refer his patients "temporarily" to another psychiatrist.

One afternoon about a month after he'd come in, we finally had a breakthrough of sorts. We had been laughing over Graham

Greene's *Our Man In Havana*. Dave was starting to have problems seeing, but he had read it before and I quoted some of the funny parts to him. When I bent to give him a hug and say goodbye for the day, he hugged me back and then asked me to stay a little longer.

"Sure, Dave, what is it?"

"I'm not going to live, am I?"

I couldn't think of one comforting, therapeutic thing to say. I just looked at him hopelessly. He continued, "You don't have to say it. I know what this disease is doing to me. And really it is almost a relief, because I don't want to live like this."

"Dave, have you read that book I bought you? You have to fight it. You have to eat better and meditate and visualize!"

"I'll try. I really will."

Later, I realized that I cut him off when he was finally ready and needed to talk. I would not let him talk about what it was like to be dying. I'd worried about him being in denial about his illness, but it ended up that I had the hardest time accepting the situation. It didn't seem possible that this beautiful, loving person would actually die. He'd just started a new practice and he was going to make such a positive difference in so many people's lives. Why couldn't someone else die? Someone who didn't care about making the world a better place? I couldn't believe that Dave could even suggest that there could be a loving God!

*   *   *

The next week Dave became very confused and agitated and was diagnosed with meningitis, which is also typical with AIDS. He had to go to the intensive care unit. And it just so happened that the day he went to the unit was Halloween and all the nurses on my floor

Patricia Taylor

had decided it would be fun to dress up for the patients. So I had to help transport Dave to I.C.U., dressed in a white apron over a red puffy-sleeved dress, with pigtails and red ribbons sticking out from the sides of my head, and my cheeks painted with big red dots, brown spots over my nose, and bright red enlarged lips. I'm not sure what I was supposed to "be" but I know that being it was one of the more humiliating moments of my life. It was as if I didn't have a clue as to how serious this was for Dave. Luckily for me, Dave smiled at my get-up and even let one of the other nurses get a picture of us together. It's the only picture I have of him.

He stayed in I.C.U. for a few days, and then returned to our unit with a "No Code" order. This meant that if he stopped breathing we were not to do anything "heroic," but were just to let him go. Apparently the physician had talked to Dave's sister on the phone and decided that this was best. We would just be trying to keep him as comfortable as possible.

He was what is called semi-comatose, meaning he would moan out when we turned him or did anything else painful, but he did not respond to us in any other way. We fed him through a tube and let his urine come out through a tube. We gave him oxygen through a mask over his face, we changed his position often, and we cleaned him up after his bowel movements. It seemed like he was already gone. Then came that day when Cheryl and I turned him and he asked, "When did we have sex on the beach?"

I was excited. But, other than asking this twice, he said nothing. Those were the last words that Dave spoke: "Sex on the beach. When did we have sex on the beach?"

*   *   *

I was surprised to find the chapel packed for the funeral. I found a seat near the back. *Where were all of these people while Dave was is the hospital?* Most were men who looked his age. A few introduced themselves and told me that I had meant a lot to Dave. Did he tell his friends about me? Did he tell them not to come to the hospital so that no one would suspect that he was gay?

Several of the men stood up during the service and talked about what a good friend and colleague Dave had been to them. One young woman stood and said, "Dr. Faulkner was my doctor and I felt so hopeful that he was really going to be able to help me because he cared." I wanted to say how comforting Dave had been to me, but I was too shy to stand in front of all those people.

Finally, another woman stood to give her farewell. She looked like she was in her 40's; she was probably about 10 years older than Dave. She had on a conservative brown dress and her dull, brown hair looked like a helmet, from too much hairspray. She introduced herself as Ellie, Dave's sister.

"We are here to celebrate that Davy, my baby brother, has gone to be with the Lord. He told me the last time we talked on the phone that he had accepted Jesus as his savior, so I know that he is in heaven now. I want to encourage all of you to accept Jesus like Davy did."

A Christian? I thought about this while she talked. I knew that Dave believed in a loving God, but I didn't realize that he had become a Christian. Despite his talking about St. Augustine, he had also talked about Buddha, Hindu gods, and American Indian gods and Muslim mystics. I was glad that he had found something that had given him peace throughout his illness, although it definitely surpassed my understanding.

I woke up from my reverie to hear her end with: "God took

him on home. I'm so grateful to know that he is finished with his sinful, disgusting lifestyle. His life was a total waste here until he repented. Thank God he did." She returned to her seat.

Someone behind me gasped. I slunk down in my pew, as if guilty for listening. A man in front of me sat up straighter in protest. The silence in the church was stifling for what seemed like hours, until the minister asked us to stand for the final prayer.

What she said, I thought later, made about as much sense as Dave asking when we'd had sex on the beach. Even less. A lot less.

Nuances of Pain

I'm up to my ears in narcotics.

Shannon gets Demerol 75 milligrams every two hours and Hayley gets Morphine 2 milligrams every two hours. They are on different schedules so someone gets something every hour, if they ask for it and they always do.

Shannon is 15 years old and her pain is located around her eyes, is dull and throbbing and is always a "ten" on the pain scale before each dose, and is an "eight" or "nine" after the medication. Then she sleeps in her room alone for two hours until she asks for the next dose.

Hayley is 12 years old and her pain is "all over but worse in my legs," very sharp and also always a "ten" before medication. After the injection it becomes a "2" or "3." Sometimes she sleeps between doses but often she reads, or colors, or watches television. Her mother is always with her.

*   *   *

"I've never worked pediatrics before, and I've certainly never given this much narcotics to children before. I usually give these kinds of medications to adults who are dying when no one worries about drug addiction."

I'm sitting on an old red plastic chair with my legs propped up on another chair the same color in the nurse's lounge. My feet are throbbing and I'm so hungry that I'm devouring a cold hamburger from the canteen machine. I have been assigned to the pediatric floor for a few weeks as the regular ped nurse is on vacation. One of the other regular ped nurses, Don, had asked me how I liked being on the pediatric floor.

"Yeah," he replied. " These kids are a lot sicker than people think. Especially the sickle cell kids."

I stuff another bite into my mouth and chew quickly. "Well, I understand that Hayley is really sick. Isn't she in what is called a *sickle cell crisis*?

"Yeah, it's really painful. Her blood cells are forming into weird shapes and clumping together and making it hard for her to get blood and oxygen to her tissues. She won't need narcotics once she gets better. She just needs some fluids, oxygen, rest, and T.L.C. and she'll go home and be O.K. for awhile. We see her about every year or so. I can't hardly stand to see her come back in so much pain." Don is a big great looking guy with wavy black hair and a neat mustache. He is eating a colorful pasta vegetable thing that he fixed for himself at home.

"Yeah, it's bad," I agree, but not wanting to imagine her pain, I change the subject. "But, what about Shannon? I can't understand that at all. She has sinusitis . . . a sinus infection right?"

Joe nods knowingly and takes a sip of bottled juice. "And, this is something she has had for years. We see her about every six months for antibiotics. Always the same thing. And it's not like she's going to get better in a few days and not need any more narcotics. She has to be addicted by now. She has a doc who gives her whatever she wants. We tried placebos but she complained so much about 'the lowered dose' that she went back on the Demerol."

"Sounds like she's really manipulating things." I throw my hamburger wrapper into a can nearby, wishing I had something sweet to finish the meal with.

"Yeah, and we don't have much choice. If she doesn't get what she wants, she calls her dad who is some kind of a big wig. He calls the administrator, who calls us. So we just give her what she wants and let her sleep all day in there by herself."

"No one visits?"

"Nope, the only time we hear from family is when her dad calls. He has a woman who comes to get her when Shannon goes home on release."

*   *   *

Things have quieted down on this floor, for some reason. It is my third day on peds, and Hayley and Shannon are still getting their drugs but Hayley is not asking for hers as often and Shannon is a little more patient when I am a few minutes late.

I've taken to sitting with Shannon every time I can. I've just given her the Demerol, and instead of going back to sleep, she agrees to sit up and try and eat her lunch. I haven't seen her eat more than a few bites in the last 2 days and she already looks so very thin. The green hospital gown has fallen down over her shoulder and her bones stick out in her chest. I help her tie the gown back up, arrange the lunch tray in front of her, and then sit on the edge of her bed.

Shannon pours several packets of ketchup over her hot dog and fries, looks at them dubiously, and then picks up the hot dog and licks off the ketchup that has run out over the bun. I observe that she is really a pretty child; I hadn't noticed before with her always under the covers and her hair a ratted mess. But her hair is a pretty blond red and her cute nose is covered with freckles. She doesn't take a bite of the meat or bun.

Patricia Taylor

"What do you usually eat at home?" I ask; wondering if I can order something that she likes.

"Oh, whatever, usually just cereal or something. We don't make a big deal about meals in our house." She has already put her hot-dog down and is sipping on her Pepsi. Finally she fingers a French fry. I sit quietly while she finally raises the ketchup covered fry, puts it into her mouth, and chews slowly.

"Who lives with you?" I ask, really curious about her life at home.

"Well, Dad of course, but he's not there much. And Mable, my sitter. She doesn't care about much though. Mom died when I was 5 and Mable's lived with us ever since. She lets me do whatever I want."

Shannon picks up another fry and eats it too. She even reaches for another ketchup package and spreads more over the rest of the potatoes.

"Who else do you spend time with? Friends?"

"No, not really. I'm too sick to go to school most of the time and Mable doesn't really like other kids to come to the house. But, I don't really care. I just hurt so much all the time that all I want to do is sleep anyway." She stops eating and looks so sad, but then she smiles. "Sometimes Dad takes me out for a movie or something when I feel better and we have fun. He's really a good Dad." Her green eyes light up for a second.

I smile with her, wanting to hang on to that second when she looks like a happy child. But then she frowns, puts her hand to her forehead, and says her head hurts too much to eat more.

I help her to the bathroom to brush her teeth and then to get comfortable in bed. I stroke her hair until she dozes off.

*   *   *

Nuances of Pain

Hayley smiles a great deal now and needs less and less pain medication. She is small for her age and really acts a lot younger than 12 too. Her black hair is plaited tightly to her head and her skin is dark brown. She sits on her bed with several dolls around her while her father reads to all of them. School books are lined up on the bedside table and I know she does lessons everyday with her mother.

"How did you do with your dinner?" I interrupt.

"Good, my nanny sent me soup and corn bread. I ate it all." She and her father both smile proudly.

"Alright! You'll be out of here before you know it. Where is your mom?"

"In the play room. Trying to get some rest," the father replies. He looks like he needs rest too. He wears a blue-gray suit and has come in right after work. He gives me a sad smile and I notice wrinkles around his eyes and forehead.

I look in on Hayley's mother. She isn't sleeping, but sitting on a green-blue plaid sofa, and she beckons me to join her.

I sit down beside her and smile. "Hayley seems to be feeling pretty good."

"Yes, praise the Lord, the worst seems to be over now." She leans back. She is a young chubby black woman with her hair wound up in amazing braids. The areas under her eyes are dark and her eyes droop. She hasn't had much sleep in a week now.

"This crisis has been really hard on all of you." I lean forward and look into her dark eyes.

"Honey, you don't know. Crisis doesn't begin to describe it. Hayley is our only baby. We are afraid to have any more because of the sickle cell." Her eyes start to tear. "We are so afraid of losing her. And we don't understand why a child like her has to suffer. She'll never have a normal life and she'll just get sicker and sicker."

Patricia Taylor

I put my hand over hers, and stay quiet not knowing what to say. I know nothing could possibly help. This isn't just a child in an acute crisis. This is a family in chronic crisis. It won't really get better just because Hayley feels good now and is going home.

* * *

Shannon has washed and combed her hair and pretty red curls surround her neck. She is wearing her own frilly bright- blue long sleeved nightgown and looks like a princess. She says her pain is only a "6" today, so she agreed to the grooming. Now Shannon is propped up in the bed with several pillows and I am reading to her from a children's book that I found in the playroom. It is for children much younger than Shannon but she told me that she loves dogs, and this is a book about how a dog showed Santa Claus the true meaning of Christmas. She even giggles some.

Then Shannon's mood turns serious. "I've wanted a puppy for as long as I can remember. But Mable doesn't want to deal with it." She rolls her green eyes to the ceiling. "She says she'll have to do all the work. But, I swear I'd love it and take care of it," she says emphatically.

I nod, really identifying with her wanting a puppy. "Does your Dad know you want a dog?"

"Yes, but he says it's up to Mable, and I can have one when I'm on my own. That seems like forever," she whines. "And, how will I take care of myself if I never get better? My teacher says if I don't get better, I'll never finish school, and I'll never go to college."

"Would you like to go to college?"

"I don't know. I just want to be able to have a puppy. Dad says that he'll always be here to take care of me. But that might mean

Mabel will live with us forever and I'll never have a puppy."

I nod again, thinking that as long as her dad enables her to use narcotics on a daily basis, she really isn't going to get better.

*   *   *

Hayley and Shannon both went home today. Hayley left waving to us as she walked out between her smiling parents. Shannon went in a wheelchair with Mable, her sitter, carrying Shannon's antibiotic and narcotic prescriptions for home. Shannon looked sad, but brightened a few minutes when I deposited a large stuffed orange poodle on her lap. The toy had a blue hat that announced 'I love you."

Hayley was the child who came in "in a life threatening crisis." And though the crisis is over for now, there is no end in sight for her or her family.

And Shannon came in with just a chronic problem that shouldn't end her life and no one worried about too much. She wasn't considered to be in crisis. But come to find out, she too is in crisis, the crisis of being unloved, and also with no end in sight.

Patricia Taylor

Just a Nurse

"*N*o, this is not *my* mother," Anna pronounced as she jumped
out of her chair, flinging her arms and long frizzy hair. I jerked back
and spilled warm coffee on my lap. She continued while I fanned my
skirt with my clipboard, trying to cool off. "One month ago she was
running an interior decorator business and now she's paralyzed and
can't even breathe on her own?" She started to pace around her chair,
knocking into the coffee table, almost spilling coffee again, and bump-
ing a large potted palm behind her chair. "God, it just doesn't work
this way. This doesn't happen to people like her. There is no way she
has this disease they say she has and is really in this bad of shape!
She's strong and things like this don't get her down like they do other people." She stopped pacing and stood over me, glaring, with her
hands on her hips. "And you're going to sit calmly and ask me what
happened to my mother?"

I *had* asked Anna what had led up to her mother being hos-
pitalized. And I had been sitting and must have appeared pretty calm
before the coffee incident. But she had appeared calm too. We were
alone in the family visiting area. The room was painted a forest green
and we sat in big gold over–stuffed chairs surrounded by lots of green-
ery and pictures of wild animals.

I thought that she was coping amazingly well considering the
situation; her mother had just been admitted to our acute long-care
facility with body paralysis and the diagnosis of Guillain-Barre Syn-
drome. I brought us some fresh cups of great smelling coffee and we
had chatted some. She was also a nurse and worked in the hospital

across town, where she cared for women in labor and helped to deliver their babies. "Just an O.B. nurse," was all she had said about that. I guessed she was 40 something and she reported that she was "single and childless; I like it that way."

Anna wore a long brown wrinkled cotton dress and clunky Birkenstocks. She wasn't wearing makeup and looked like she might never. Her cheeks were red, chubby, and dimpled and her smile was so great-when she smiled.

But now she was glaring at me with round hazel eyes, obviously furious at my insensitivity. "You want to know what happened?" she repeated, as she sunk back down into her chair.

I nodded, lowering my eyes to my interview form while she leaned forward and continued with her animated hands in the air. "She was fine! Wilma—that's what she wants to be called- was working a lot and doing great. In fact we hadn't hardly seen her in weeks because she was doing some big mansion down on the river, the guy wanted it ready for his new wife, which he didn't get, 'cause that Doctor Moore insisted on putting Mother in the hospital."

Anna stopped to push her long gray streaked mousy brown hair behind her neck and to take a deep breath. Then she sat back in the chair and continued a little more slowly as if trying to calm herself. "She *was* having some tingling in her legs and she was so weak it was hard for her to walk but I think with a few days of rest she would have been fine. She had Dad take her to the clinic just to see if she could get a vitamin B-12 shot or something. No way did she want to be admitted: her business depends on her being reliable." She gave me a pointed look and edged up suddenly to the front of the chair again. "But that idiot doctor made Dad just pick her up and carry her to the car and drive her to the emergency room." Anna was waving her arms and talking rapidly again.

Patricia Taylor

"Dad said that she kept yelling that she didn't need to go to the hospital but he was afraid not to do what the doctor said. I don't know why he didn't call me." She was going to start bawling. I wished she'd stop and take another breath.

"And she ended up in the I.C.U. The stress of the whole thing just made it worse. Wilma got so weak she couldn't even complain about being there, and then they said she was about to stop breathing on her own and needed a respirator. I swear if they'd just left her alone . . ."

Finally, Anna stopped. After a few moments she rearranged her face into a bleak smile and picked up what was left of her coffee for a small sip. I had started to reach out to comfort her, but went back to holding my clipboard. (I was afraid to try anymore of what was left of my own coffee and maybe appear unconcerned.)

"And now I guess we are *here*." She rolled her eyes as if she thought the situation was ridiculous and then frowned at me again. "Her insurance wouldn't pay for any more intensive care, but they'd pay for this. Isn't that nuts?"

I assumed this was a rhetorical question and kept my mouth closed. Acute long term care was for people who needed a lot more time to heal than what was realistic in an I.C U. bed.

"I understand that your specialty is rehabilitation," she said in an ironic tone. I nodded a little and she continued, now more agitated again. "Well, she damn well better get better. I'm on leave to stay with her around the clock to make sure she does. She's got to get back to work; there are a lot of people who need her."

Anna put her coffee down roughly, producing a hollow sound, and sighed heavily. She ran both hands up over her face, through her hair again, and down the back of her neck. Sighing again, she leaned back into her chair with her eyes closed. I was thinking about her words, "I'm on leave to stay with her. I'll be here around the clock." Then she sat up and continued in a bewildered voice. "I don't even remember learning about Guillain-Barre in nursing school."

I didn't remember learning about that particular disease in nursing school either, but I wasn't about to admit that. In fact, I didn't really want to say anything for fear of Anna getting angry again.

She reached for her blue-gray knit bag on the floor, removed a folded yellow legal pad sheet, unfolded it, and looked at it. "I understand that the cause is not known but it's sometimes initiated with a virus or a bacterial infection." She looked up at me. "Mother didn't have that; she's never been sick a day in her life." She stopped for a second to make sure that I got that. I nodded and made a note on my clipboard. She read on, "It's an inflammatory process that breaks down the lining of the peripheral nerves. As in Mother's case, it starts in the lower extremities and then spreads up the body until it affects the lungs." She gave me a meaningful glance. I nodded, not daring to say that I was her mother's nurse and hopefully knew all this by now.

"Anyway," Anna put the yellow sheet back into her bag, slung it over her shoulder, and stood up. She pushed back her hair dramatically, tying it into a big loose knot behind her neck. "This disease is supposed to reverse itself in the opposite direction, from head to toe." She gave me a determined look. "So, the first thing to do is get her off the respirator. I've got to go talk to the respiratory therapist." And with a nod of her head, she swept out of the room, as well as a person can sweep out of a room in Birkenstocks.

I sat stunned. Then, I recorded the few details she had supplied about her mother's symptoms, the fact that the daughter was a nurse and well informed about her mother's illness, and the presumption that Anna and her family would need a great deal of emotional support.

*   *   *

Anna's mother, Wilma, lay propped up in a vinyl beige recliner with a clear-white plastic respirator hose extending from her neck and crossing her chest to the large noisy machine behind her. She was a small woman with obviously dyed blond hair with darker blond roots. But she still looked stylish. And, really, she didn't look much older than Anna.

Wilma was in our high observation area, which contained four hospital beds. Three other people, also on respirators, shared this room. Each had a monitor above the bed that showed oxygen levels and vital signs. A white curtain extended from the ceiling around each bed and could be pulled for privacy. The nurse's station was a round table in the middle of the room and was covered with medical records, a fax machine, a phone, and a computer. A locked cart by the door contained medications and other equipment.

Wilma had been on our unit for two weeks and was into a regular routine. I had performed her physical assessment, which involved looking, listening, and feeling from her head to her toes. Then I had given her morning medication with her tube feeding via the gastrostomy tube that extended from her stomach through her abdominal wall. The nursing assistant had already given her a bed bath, and a physical therapist had exercised all her extremities and lifted her into her chair. A respiratory therapist was in and out frequently and was in the process of weaning Wilma from the respirator: Four times a day she was taken off the respiratory setting and given two hours to breathe on her own with just a little pressurized oxygen to help her. She was tolerating all of her therapy well, and we hoped she'd soon be off the respirator, feeding herself and moving her legs. She frequently smiled and never complained, which was highly unusual.

When Wilma was on the respirator, I held up a large poster board with pictures of things that Wilma would be likely to want such as a bedpan, a cool mouth rinse, or a position change. She could point to these items until she was off the respirator and able to speak for herself. Her arms were so weak that she could barely reach the board but she was gaining strength and getting better. And she did get off the respirator in a few days without any real problems.

And then, a few days after that, she asked for a brush. She wanted me to help her groom for her husband's visit during his lunch hour.

"O.K. We'll give you the works.," I said. I got out her big pink *Mary Kay* makeup case. She smiled and nodded.

I ran a brush through Wilma's thick wavy hair that was cut bluntly around her heart-shaped face; she looked how I assumed Barbie, the doll, would if she ever became 65. I knew that Wilma literally expected 'the works,' as Anna had given me detailed instructions on how to care for Wilma. Anna had gone home to do the laundry. So I brushed hair and colored eyebrows, eyelashes, cheeks and lips (all products in pink containers) Then I got out her baby blue lacy bed jacket and put it loosely around her shoulders. That brought out the blue in her eyes. She really did look like a doll.

I covered her faded hospital gown, urine bag, thin weak legs, blue socks and Reebok walking shoes with a silky pastel blanket. Wilma loosely pointed to the bedside table with her Bible. I spread the Bible in front of her. Anna had left a note about what pages Wilma would read that day. I put her navy reading glasses on her nose and over her ears. I guessed even Barbie would wear glasses, or more likely contacts, by that age. She smiled again and mouthed 'Thank You.'

Soon after that, Wilma's husband ambled in. He was also blond and darn if he didn't resemble Ken. I had the impression that the original Ken was a lot more outgoing though. He sat in a chair near Wilma and read the *Wall Street Journal*, occasionally helping her turn the pages in the Bible. I was thinking she would probably be getting tired by now but she didn't indicate this in any way, and physical therapy wasn't planning on putting her back to bed for another hour.

Suddenly Anna burst into the room. She carried a large garbage bag full of bed jackets (a different color for each day) with matching socks that she had washed for her mother, as well as her own new supply of wrinkled clothes for the next week. Wilma winced when she saw the garbage bag. I assumed *she* wouldn't carry clothes around this way. But Anna seemed proud of her accomplishment and smiled as she unpacked each item and threw it in the closet. Then she turned her attention on her mother and saw Wilma's second definite wince. The smile left Anna's face.

"Wilma, have you had your pain medicine yet?" she asked as she leaned down to give her mother a kiss on the cheek. Wilma shook her head. Anna spun towards me. "She hasn't had her pain medicine?" I shook my head. She spun again, to her father. "Dad, you were supposed to remind the nurses to keep her medicated. You know how her back hurts her so much, especially when she's up in a chair."

"She didn't look like she was hurting," we both blurted at the same time.

"You both know, I've told you, that you can't tell if a person is in pain just by how they look. In a situation like this you just know this is going to hurt," she yelled at both of us. We sheepishly looked at Wilma. Wilma didn't confirm or deny anything from the way she smiled at us.

"Do you need medication, Wilma?" I asked.

"No," she finally said, shaking her head.

Anna looked like she wanted to argue, but then she sat down on her mother's bed and sulkily wound her hair in a knot around her head. Wilma gave Anna a look of pity, and then continued her Bible reading.

Since Wilma was successfully weaned from the ventilator and progressing in her healing, she sent her daughter back to work. So, the other staff and I had had most days alone with Wilma for the last two weeks except for "Ken's" lunch visits.

I helped Wilma to sit up in her bed and prepare for breakfast. I opened her juice, put a spoon in her hand, and poured milk over her oatmeal. Though still very weak, she had been able to feed herself with this help.

I sat a few minutes at the desk to record my morning assessments. Suddenly there was an obnoxious beep and a clash of dishes falling to the floor. I jerked my head up to see Wilma flailing about the bed. Undigested orange juice and oatmeal were dripping from her mouth and running down her gown. Her face was purple and her monitor showed that her heart rate and oxygen levels were dropping rapidly.

I ran to her as she struggled to breathe. Her eyes were large with panic. I grabbed a package from the bedside table with a suction tube and sterile gloves. I pushed 'on' to the wall suction device and donned the gloves. I inserted the suction tube into Wilma's nose and down into her trachea. With the opening on my end of the tube occluded, I twisted and withdrew the tube while counting to 10 so she wouldn't be without oxygen longer than that. Yellow fluid flowed in the tube toward the wall canister. I suctioned several times until Wilma took some deep breaths. Her eyes started to relax. I grabbed a mask from the wall, turned on the oxygen and placed it over Wilma's mouth and nose.

Her respirations slowed and became regular. The monitor showed that her heart rate and oxygen levels also returned to normal.

My heart rate and breathing were steadying too. We looked at each other for a long time, somehow intimate after our shared moment of fear.

Later, as I helped her wash and change clothes, we talked some about what had happened. "I think I was just trying to eat too fast. I want so badly to get better." It was the only time she ever admitted to feeling any sense of weakness. "Please don't tell Anna or Ken about this."

"I promise I won't tell." *As if this is something to be ashamed of.*

*　　*　　*

Wilma had moved to her own private room. Anna came faithfully to spend every night and one of her days off with her mother. On her other day off she stayed away to do the laundry and any shopping Wilma needed. She and Wilma never talked about Anna's obstetrical nursing job, I noticed. But Wilma spent lots of time explaining the interior decorating business to her daughter who seemed enthralled by it all.

Wilma had just settled into her chair and arranged her planning calendar, pens, magazines, phone book and phone around her. She had decided to drum up some business via the phone, though her doctor had told her that she shouldn't go back to work for several months.

Anna, on her evening off, rushed in with a large *Wendy's* milkshake. "Here, Wilma, I brought you a snack," She bent over for the usual kiss on her mother's cheek. Wilma blew a kiss at Anna, apparently not wanting to smear her perfectly applied fuchsia lipstick. She smiled indulgently at her daughter. "Dear, you know I don't eat things like that."

"You are supposed to be getting extra calories and protein so you can keep building your strength," Anna said in a whining voice.

"You all gave me plenty of protein and calories while I couldn't make my own choices. It's a miracle I didn't gain 20 pounds." Wilma looked so small in her yellow short and top outfit with matching socks and her neatly tied Reeboks, like a teenager getting ready to play tennis. In fact, she was getting closer to being able to play tennis. She still needed her walker for support, but she was getting all over the place by herself and definitely gaining strength, without take-out food..

Anna fell into a chair near her mother. She started to suck noisily on the straw of the milkshake. Wilma rolled her eyes but didn't say anything. I had heard this argument and seen the same outcome more than once.

*   *   *

At the end of the day I went into Wilma's room to say goodbye. She smiled from her phone book and waved distractedly. Anna was standing in front of the open closet.

"Wilma, where is all the dirty laundry?" Anna asked innocently." I need to do it tomorrow." She stood there for a few minutes obviously taking in the fact that not only was the large garbage bag gone from the bottom of the closet, but stacks of clean clothes were folded neatly on the top shelves.

She turned to her mother who was intently dialing a number on a nearby phone. "Wilma, did you hear me? What happened to the laundry?"

Wilma covered the mouthpiece of the phone with her hand and whispered to Anna, "Wait a minute, dear."

Anna looked liked she had been struck. She stood still a second and then lunged at Wilma and the phone. "Get off the friggin phone and tell me what happened to the God Damn laundry!" Wilma's eyes got enormous as she dropped the phone at Anna's approach.

The phone spun on the floor and I grabbed for it, saying 'Hello?' into the speaker "It's dead," I pronounced foolishly.

They both glared at me, and Anna continued, "Wilma, where is the laundry?"

"I did it myself, dear," Wilma replied, composing her facial muscles into a calm smile. "The nice girl in occupational therapy took me down to the laundry room and made me do a load of laundry to see if I was ready to manage on my own at home."

"But *I* always do the laundry!" Wilma howled.

"I know, dear, but, really I did fine and I might as well do my own laundry from now on."

I expected Anna to quiet down and sulk, as she usually did, but she started to sob. She knelt down on the floor and put her head on her mother's bedside table. Her head bobbed for what seemed like forever. I put a hand on her shoulders. Finally, she rocked back on to her heels and rubbed her hands over her face. I handed her a few Kleenex from the table and she blew her nose.

"Mom . . ." She started woefully.

"Wilma." Wilma reminded her primly.

Anna sighed deeply. "*Wilma* . . . The only thing you've ever let me do for you is the laundry."

"You don't have to do anything for me. I'm strong and I can take care of myself."

"Yes, *Wilma*, I know." Her voice was shrill. "You are strong, and perfect and a genius and I'm just shit." Anna leaned over again onto herself and covered her face and shoulders with her long dull frizzy hair.

Wilma smiled indulgently. "Now, Dear, You need to trust the Lord. You better go home and pray and get yourself under control."

Anna pulled herself up, her hair still covering her face. Without looking at either of us, she slunk out of her mother's room.

*　　*　　*

The day of Wilma's discharge she wore a short navy summer suit, a silky red blouse and pearl earrings. The only thing missing was the heels; the physical therapist insisted that she wear her walking shoes. Also she still needed a tri-pod cane for support, but if she hadn't had the shoes and cane she would have looked like she was heading straight to an important business meeting. Even her hair had been trimmed and colored by her personal stylist who had made a trip to the hospital. Anna had gone to the business office to settle financial matters and Wilma awaited her as she sat on the edge of her chair with all of her belongings packed around her.

I had not seen Anna since the day of the laundry crisis. I had been off on a week's vacation, but other nurses had told me that Anna had been staying with her mother again for the last two nights. "Wait until you see her, you won't believe it," they had all said.

And sure enough, I didn't believe it. Anna walked into her mother's room wearing a black linen dress with black heels. And her hair was cut and colored a dark auburn. It curled beautifully around the top of her shoulders. She was even wearing makeup; you couldn't see her freckles anymore and she had on mascara and coral lipstick. Wilma smiled and nodded approvingly as Anna dipped to exchange air kisses with her mother.

"Dear, you look wonderful. See if you can find us a cart for all this stuff," Wilma drawled as she swept her arm over all her belongings.

"I'll get you one," I offered and left the room in search of a cart. Anna came after me.

"You'll never guess what has happened," she said brightly, smiling her rare gorgeous smile.

I stopped and turned back to her. "What?"

"Mom . . . I mean Wilma . . ." she stopped to giggle, "has decided to train me to be her assistant. Since she's really not supposed to be working yet and she does expect her business to keep growing. She'll need help."

I tried to keep my face expressionless.

"Isn't that cool?" Except for her frequent whining, I had never noticed before how much she sounded like a child.

"What about your nursing career?"

"Oh, I just gave my notice. No big deal. I'm just an O. B. nurse. Anyone can do what I've been doing."

"Oh," I replied. I turned to look for the cart, not sure what else to do or say.

Anyone can help women through the greatest experience of their lives? Anyone can help an infant to survive? Anyone can help families adjust to major new roles? Anyone can help a grieving parent of an ill or dead infant? Anyone can be an O.B. nurse? Anyone can assess a patient and make life saving decisions in a moment? Anyone can be a nurse?

I smiled, while inwardly rolling my eyes, as I drove an empty cart and a wheelchair into the room and prepared them for discharge. Wilma magisterially took her seat in the wheelchair and was wheeled out. The cart piled high with plants, flowers, and possessions in expensive pink suitcases came next. Finally came Anna, in tow, still awkward in her high-heeled shoes and fumbling sophistication.

A Wonderful Job at Dove Lane

I've finally found it. 1920 Dove Lane is an expansive piece of perfectly landscaped property surrounding a massive, modern, gorgeous house. In the large circle drive between the house and the unattached garage, I park my dusty Nissan van behind two bright colorful cars that look like the cars I've seen on *Rich and Famous* TV. I'm nervous because I'm not used to visiting this type of neighborhood. My hospice area usually consists of farm houses that are small and need a lot of repairs. But I remind myself that when people are in pain it doesn't matter how much money they have, and so I head toward the front door with a vow do to a wonderful job to relieve any suffering in this home.

I am met by a very attractive blond woman in her early thirties. She is dressed to attend an elegant woman's tea party with a pink silky dress and a large pink straw hat. I think that this is probably her destination because I have watched *Dallas*. She introduces herself as Candice, Mr. Howard's wife, and leads me through the house to meet him.

The multiple large rooms are, of course, perfectly decorated and very spacious. The colors are all white and light pastels. Large picture windows and flowered plants in every room add to the effect of being in a sunny garden. I can see a large pool with an attached Jacuzzi outside, and a lake with ducks farther behind that. Everything is spotless; it looks as if no one really lives here. I feel very out of place in my polyester navy skirt, white cotton blouse, and practical navy blue loafers. I am carrying my over-stuffed black leather nursing bag.

Patricia Taylor

Mr. Howard, my new patient, is in a room in the far end of the house. This is unusual because Hospice patients are usually sitting up in recliners or couches in the living room when I arrive for my first visit. Or if a hospital bed has already arrived, patients will be all settled in their bed in the middle of the house where all the family activity takes place. Most people don't want to be tucked away in a back bedroom the last few months of their lives.

However, Mr. Howard is in his bedroom propped up in a king-sized bed with all of the drapes pulled. The walls are a dark wood and covered with shelves containing books and statues of horses and what looks like war heroes. The bed, windows, floor, and dark wood chairs are covered in black and brown materials and there are no plants or flowers in this room. He is surrounded by an oxygen tank, a bedside commode, a table full of history, pill bottles and some un-eaten Jell-O. This room is quite a contrast from the rest of the house. There are no indications that Candice spends any time here, let alone sleeps here.

He looks like he is in his late 40's but his record states that he is 57. He's handsome with dark brown hair and blue eyes that match his navy silk pajamas. He doesn't look thin and drawn either, like a lot of cancer patients do. He does seem awfully drowsy, though, and I notice that his pupils are constricted. He is quiet and speaks only when spoken to. He seems to feel somewhat unsure about me being there. This is sometimes the way it is at first, as patients fear that by my coming, they will die sooner.

Another woman is sitting beside him on his bed. She states that she is Susan, Candice's sister, and that she is a nurse and will be taking care of Mr. Howard. She is another pretty blond who seems very crisp and efficient and she does indeed seem to be knowledgeable about nursing skills. Candice leaves us, saying that she has an appointment. This concerns me because usually I like to interview the family members along with the patient on the first visit. Susan says that she will answer any questions that I have. I sit in a chair near the bed and review the philosophy of Hospice.

I explain that our goal is palliative, not curative. We want to help Mr. Howard to live the rest of his life with as much quality as possible. "We" includes a doctor, a social worker, a nurses' aide, a minister, some volunteers, and myself, the nurse. We want to help with control of any difficult physical symptoms, emotional issues, hygiene, and light chores and errands as necessary. And possibly more important, we want to help him and his family accept the situation and have some meaningful time together before the inevitable death.

Susan says, "We know all about Hospice, we just want better pain control. We don't need any one else to visit besides you." Mr. Howard nods an agreement. I think to myself that these must be very private people who do not want a lot of strangers in and out of their home. And I assume because Susan is available and they obviously have the financial means, they do not need as much support as many people do.

Most people of course jump at the opportunity to have a lot of help as it is very difficult for the family to take care of a dying person around the clock for several months. And for the patient it is usually helpful to have other people to talk to besides the emotionally upset and exhausted family members, who often do not want to talk about what it is like to be dying.

But for this family, I turn my attention to Mr. Howard's physical complaints which seem to be their major concern. I hope that while caring for these needs that I can offer psychological comfort also, if I can establish trust.

Susan says that Mr. Howard has constant pain in his chest because of his lung cancer, that he has been taking Methadone for pain control, and it is not helping. Methadone is a long-acting narcotic that is usually pretty effective for cancer pain.

Susan lists other complaints that include constant shortness of breath, no appetite, weakness, trouble sleeping at night and constipation. She says that he stays in bed all of the time and dozes a lot during the day. He only gets up to use the bedside commode a few times a day. I notice that he is not using his oxygen, and when I ask him about it, he says it doesn't help him. I attempt to ask him other questions about his symptoms but Susan interrupts and says he is too weak to talk much.

I listen to his lungs and note that the sounds are hard to hear on the left side which is to be expected over a tumor, but they are clear throughout the rest of the chest. And his respirations do not appear labored; in fact they are at the rate of 10 which is quite a bit below the normal of 16-20 breaths per minute. This is unusual for someone whose lungs are covered with cancer and mucous. He certainly does not appear to be in a great deal of respiratory distress.

I also wonder about the severity of his pain as it is unusual for patients to have that much pain in the chest with lung cancer. Usually the severe pain occurs in bones or other organs when the cancer spreads. But I know better than to doubt someone's pain. If it is real to them, then it is a concern for me.

I talk to him about the use of his Methadone and suggest that he try to take Tylenol or Ibuprofen between the 12 hour doses of Methadone to enhance the pain relief. Also I tell him that I will call his doctor to discuss his pain medication. Susan states that I don't need to do that as their doctor is a good friend of theirs and that they will call and get his Methadone increased. They call their doctor "Larry." Apparently Mr. Howard used to play golf with him and he has done some charity work with Candice. In fact, "Larry" will be dropping by to check on them frequently, Susan says.

While I continue to assess the rest of Mr. Howard's body, I think to myself that I will call "Larry" anyway, because this is a very strange situation. I then suggest some high calorie, high protein snacks and a daily bowel care program. I also suggest that he try to get up out of bed a little each day to increase his strength and to help him sleep better at night. I think that if nothing else, getting out of this dark room would help psychologically. I mention that he might want to try his oxygen again when he gets short of breath, particularly when he gets up. They don't seem to have much interest in my suggestions.

I ask if they have any other concerns or things that I can help with and they say no. I tell them that I will visit Mr. Howard every other week for now and that I will call later in the day to discuss the doctor's intentions concerning pain control.

As I drive to my next appointment I wonder why these people have requested Hospice. They do not seem to really want or need anything. They have good insurance and Mr. Howard is too young for Medicare; he has a way to go before he'll be 65 and eligible. Medicare would help financially with drugs and supplies at this time. They said their main concern was symptom management, primarily pain, but yet they are apparently able to get any medications they need from "Larry." They don't even want me to call this Larry, their doctor. And they certainly were not interested in my words of wisdom. Maybe Susan just wants a second nursing opinion, and will follow up on some of my suggestions. Maybe she isn't sure that having "Larry" visit frequently will be enough, as physicians don't always see things the way we nurses do.

Later when I get "Larry" on the phone he states that Mr. Howard has an inoperable tumor on the left side of his chest and that Mr. Howard has refused any further treatment. "Larry" states he has already increased the Methadone dose today, as Susan called him earlier.

He states that the Howards are very good long time friends of his and he wants them to have the VIP treatment. I think to myself that all my patients get the VIP treatment, but I keep it quiet. I ask diplomatically exactly why Mr. Howard and his family want Hospice, but "Larry" cuts me off and says again to take good care of them. "I'll hear about it if you don't," he says.

I think about how good it is to have a nice collegial relationship with the patient's physician.

*   *   *

I have been visiting Mr. Howard every other week for 6 weeks. I always determine the frequency of my visits by what I perceive as the patient and family need. Often near the end, I visit daily. I don't think that Mr. Howard needs me that much. Susan is always there with him and he doesn't seem to have really deteriorated although he is always sleeping when I arrive and is drowsy when I wake him up. He looks like he might have lost weight too and he says he still has no interest in food.

I always assess him and then give my spiel about trying to eat more, to force fluids and fiber, and to get up out of bed. Susan doesn't take any of my suggestions seriously and is doing things the same way she was when I first came. I don't seem to have developed much of a relationship with Mr. Howard either, as he is as taciturn with me as he was the first day.

I wonder if he is getting too much medication, as he is so sedated and his respirations are often between 8 and 10, but Susan says that he still has terrible pain and he needs what he is taking. Mr.

Howard nods in agreement. I call "Larry" to report on my patient's condition and he says just to keep his friend comfortable and that he will visit them on Sunday. Susan tells me that she thinks I need to start coming weekly because her brother-in-law is so much sicker.

*   *   *

I've been visiting now weekly for several weeks and there has been no real change. Today Susan calls just two days after my last visit to tell me that Mr. Howard is having severe back pain and that I need to visit ASAP. I rearrange my schedule and rush to their home wondering if something different has happened. Sometimes cancer spreads to areas that cause sudden unbearable pain, like the spine. When I arrive at the home, however, there seems to be no basis for panic. Candice is in the drive heading for the garage. She tells me that she would like to talk to me and for me to follow her to the garage where she is getting her hair done.

Sure enough, in the back of the garage is a large, classy bathroom, and Candice's hairdresser has just prepared everything she needs to cut and style Candice's hair. Candice explains that she needs to stay close to her husband because he is so ill, but she is getting her hair done in the garage so he is not disturbed by any noise.

I think that this is most unusual, and ask her what she would like to talk about. I am anxious to talk to her as she often is not home during my visits. She states that she is very upset and worried about her husband, that he is very sick and irritable, and that she thinks I need to get him more pain medication and to visit them every day. Then she puts her head under the faucet for her wash. The hairdresser gives me a sympathetic smile and pours out the shampoo.

I go ahead to the house, and meet Susan at the bedroom door.

She states that Mr. Howard has been awake all night in pain and that he is having problems breathing. When I approach the bed I notice that he is wearing his oxygen mask and oxygen is infusing at a low level. He is sleeping and his respirations are 10 and he does not appear to be in more distress than usual. When I wake him up he does not mention any new pain. After my assessment, I tell Susan that I don't think that he needs any more medication right now. She says that she will call "Larry" and get what they need. But she wants to make sure that I come back tomorrow to check on them.

When I get back to the office I have a phone message that "Larry" called and ordered Morphine to be given by an injection whenever Mr. Howard's pain was not being controlled by the Methadone. I call "Larry's" office and am informed that he can't talk to me. I give his nurse an account of Mr. Howard's condition and she promises to pass this on to the good doctor. She also tells me that "Larry" thinks that the cancer has spread and there is nothing we can do but keep Mr. Howard as comfortable as possible, which I am all for as a Hospice nurse, but I feel angry at the family and at "Larry" for taking my input so lightly.

Why am I going to their house every day if I am so little valued? I call Susan and she says she has already purchased the Morphine and given a dose and that it is helping the pain. I wonder again what the heck I am needed for.

I wait until my supervisor, Trudy, gets out of a meeting and then I go into her office to tell her my concerns about Mr. Howard. I've brought up his name and condition and some of my concerns at our weekly team meetings but no one else has shown any concern about his status, except that he won't let anyone else visit. Now I want to make a point to tell Trudy that something is most irregular here.

"He is getting way too much pain medication. He is very sedated and having respiratory depression. And he wasn't complaining of any new pain before Dr. Jones ordered Morphine today."

"Are you saying that Larry Jones is not managing Mr. Howard correctly?"

"No. I'm just concerned. I feel so frustrated because I don't know what my role is here."

"Well your role is that of the nurse, not the doctor. Dr. Jones just happens to be a very respected physician and it would not be wise of you to question his judgment. His patient is dying. So what if he gets addicted to Morphine?"

Normally I agree with this philosophy heartily but that is not really the point here. I leave her office feeling frustrated, powerless and mad as hell.

*　　*　　*

I am lying in my bed at 3 a.m. on Saturday night waiting for my beeper to go off. I never can sleep when I am on call. Families are so much more anxious at night and there really do seem to be a lot more deaths, so I am always called several times. Sometimes I am out all night. And sometimes all weekend too. Sure enough, the beeper goes off and I get up to call the answering service. The operator says that Mrs. Howard has called and that her husband is dead. I call Candice and tell her that I will be there in 30 minutes and then I start the drive.

I think about the fact that Mr. Howard seemed pretty good yesterday and I did not expect him to die so soon. He was drowsy but he still spoke to me and did not seem to have a lot of trouble breathing. He was even sipping on that milkshake I had begged him to try. I wonder about his life as I always do when a patient dies. Was it what he wanted it to be? Other than making a lot of money and being married to Candice, what was it all about for him?

When I get to the house all the inside and outside lights are on. The drive way is full of shiny expensive cars, and the house is full of smartly dressed mourners sipping coffee. Candice and Susan are sitting in the bedroom waiting for me. Mr. Howard's body is flat in bed with the covers pulled up to his chest and his hands folded together, like bodies look in the movies. Even his eyes and mouth are closed. Dead bodies usually don't look this content in real life.

Family members don't either, for that matter; Candice and Susan look very composed. They say they have already called "Larry" and want me to call the funeral home right away, which I do. This is one of the many nice things about Hospice in Florida; a coroner does not have to be called if the deceased was a Hospice patient and was already known to have a terminal illness. As a Hospice nurse I am able to say that the patient is dead and that is enough for everyone concerned.

I sit by the body and say nice things about Mr. Howard as I always do for the family's sake. They do not seem very impressed. I feel that numbness I always feel at a death. It still isn't all that real to me, even after working all these years with dying patients. Usually though, I am acutely aware of the awful pain of the family members. Even when the death is expected and people think they are ready for it, the actual death is still an awful blow. But now I'm not aware of much pain. I think to myself that these people really hide their feelings well.

After the body is removed, I tell Candice and Susan that I need to count and dispose of any remaining narcotics in the house. This is done routinely because it is a law, which I explain to them. Usually family members take this in stride, and I think are even relieved to be rid of a reminder of all the turmoil of pain control for their sick family member.

But just as Candice and Susan are different in every other way, they do not take this in stride. In fact they become very angry and indignant that I would suggest such a thing. They demand that I leave their house! I ask them to sign a release form absolving me from responsibility, which Candice does grudgingly. And I leave. I feel more bewildered than ever.

*　　*　　*

It is Monday morning after my weekend on call. I am greeted by my un-smiling supervisor, Trudy, saying that she needs to have a talk with me right away.

"Dr. Jones called me at home yesterday. He had a call from Mr. Howard's wife who says you were rude to the family when you attended the death."

"No, I wasn't rude, I just wanted to throw away the left over narcotics and they refused. They got very angry about it. I was hurt and may have been a little defensive but I don't think I was rude."

"Well, no one else has ever complained about you before, so let's drop it. Just be aware of how you might appear to others at times when you get upset."

I leave to see my other patients thinking about how much I'd like to quit this job and Trudy, but also about how much most of my patients mean to me and how I think I am making a difference for them.

*　　*　　*

It has been months since Mr. Howard died. I never heard anymore about the case. I sent my usual bereavement letter and even called Candice offering to visit, but of course she declined. And I must be honest and say I was glad she did. I'm thinking about her again today because this morning I am visiting an Episcopal church with a friend and the church is on the side of town near where I assume Candice still lives.

The church is very majestic and I feel intimidated by all of the elegantly dressed people. They do not smile, but seem very serious, and they all seem to know exactly when to kneel, and when to stand, and when to sit, and what book to read out of at any given time.

But after the service, several people greet me and one woman says that she remembers me from the night Mr. Howard died. She says she was one of the friends in the house and she remembers how upset Candice and Susan got with me, and how she thought that was strange because she knows how wonderful Hospice nurses usually are.

She tells me that she doesn't like to gossip, but she thinks I'd be interested to know that Candice inherited quite a lot of her husband's old family money and that and she and Susan have moved to Naples, which is a very exclusive town in Florida. And, she has heard rumors that "Larry" is giving up his practice in the next month and will be moving to Florida also.

Now I'm really wondering. I'm thinking that they all seemed more than a little self absorbed at the time and I resented their complaints about me. But was there a lot more going on than I suspected? Were Candice, Susan, and "Larry" using me and the Hospice organization to meet their own ends? Was Mr. Howard's tumor really inoperable? Did he really refuse further treatment? Was he really in that much pain? Was he ever drug-free enough to make any of his own decisions? Did Susan really give the doses I thought she was giving? Why were there no other family members or friends around during his illness? Was I there simply to enable a very well conceived and constructed murder?

If so, I did a wonderful job at Dove Lane.

Patricia Taylor

Mama

I was let into the front room of the home by a tall attractive young woman with wild red curly hair who whispered to me, "We are glad you made it on time." She was dressed in bright red pajamas, robe, and feathery slippers, and looked like she hadn't slept all night, or maybe for several nights. I took two steps into the dark house ahead of her, and immediately let out an "Ouch" as I had walked into something that shot pains through both knees.

"Please try to be quiet," a man's voice whispered fiercely, "Mama is finally resting." I stood a few minutes adjusting to the dark after the bright summer sunlight while the woman closed the door behind me.

When I could make out shapes, I saw that I had bumped into a king-sized bed. It had taken a while to see because the windows were covered with dark blankets. Several people were sitting in chairs looking towards what must have been the patient in the middle of the bed. I could barely make out a thin face and messy gray hair under piles of blankets.

The young woman motioned for me to follow her around the bed and out into a dark hall. A man, even taller and more tired looking, followed us and we ended up in a kitchen with light from the sliding glass porch. I found out that they were Ed and Marcie, the son and daughter-in-law, and we all stood at the breakfast bar while I tried to get a nursing history.

We couldn't sit at the table because all of the chairs were in service of the people keeping watch on the patient in the next room.

The table was covered with a computer and piles of books and papers. I assumed one of them ran some sort of business from home.

Ed was dressed in shorts and a Florida State football T-shirt, and had dark areas under his eyes. "We've been up the last several nights with Mama. We could really use some help now that she is almost at the end," he said while they both leaned eagerly towards me.

"Tell me a little bit about what is going on with your mother," I gently commanded in my most therapeutic voice.

"She's comatose, with complete renal failure, and she's close to cardiac arrest." Ed answered, straightening up. "She hasn't gotten out of bed or eaten in days, she's had no urine output, her heart rate is barely present, and she probably has no blood pressure. We just want her to be as comfortable as possible at the end. I've been doing research so I know what to expect."

"When was the last time she was seen by a doctor?"

"Oh, it's been probably six months. She has deteriorated so much since then, and she is too sick to go see him, so he referred Mama to your Hospice doctor."

"Has Dr. Wood seen your mother?"

"No. You are supposed to report to him," Ed advised me.

"When was your mother diagnosed with Alzheimer's disease?"

"Oh, our doctor just told us that that is what Mama had last time we saw him. She'd been acting confused for a few months before that. She repeated a lot of things over and over, it was awful. And she started to get lost when she drove. We were afraid what she might do, so we had her move in with us as soon as we got the diagnosis." Ed looked down putting his hands to his head as he pushed back his greasy red hair several times, and Marcie put her arm around his shoulder and slowly nodded her agreement.

Patricia Taylor

"Does your mother have any other illness beside Alzheimer's that could be life threatening to her now?" I asked. She sounded like she was in the early stages if she was just starting to get confused about eight months ago and she certainly shouldn't be bedridden yet.

"No, she has always been in perfect health until now, but this is definitely killing her. I think we are talking only a couple of days."

"I'm so sorry. This must be so hard on you and all your family," I said this just because that's what I always said on my first visit and I always assume it must be true.

"Are those other people in the other room family?"I asked.

Marcie nodded sadly and said, "Yes, Ed's aunt and uncle are here, and my sister, and our two daughters."

After more questions from me and assurances from Ed and Marcie that they wanted their mother to die in their king-sized bed, I suggested that I see their mother.

"But Mama is finally resting," Marcie said with exasperation. "Do you have to disturb her? We had such a bad night."

"What happened?"

"She was just so restless, and kept moaning, and we finally gave her one of my Phenergan suppositories from the last time I was nauseated and that has helped her sleep. We'd like you to get us something to help her rest."

"Sure, I can ask Dr Wood about that. I do need though to check her, so that I can really give him a complete report. It's the only way to make sure she gets the best care."

"Well O.K." Ed said hesitantly, "but don't take too long."

As we headed back to the living room I asked if we could have some light so I could see their mother, so Ed turned on a lamp near the bed while the adults got up out of their chairs to make room for me to approach the bed. I noticed the children, both of them about 8 or 9, possibly twins with identical carrot red hair, looking sleepy and staring mournfully at their grandmother. Apparently they were kept out of school to be present at their grandmother's death bed.

"Why don't all of you take a break while I'm here?" I suggested. "Girls, you look like you'd feel better going outside for a little while." The girls jumped up, apparently grateful for permission, and ran towards the back of the house, while the three adults followed slowly and murmured among themselves. Ed and Marcie stayed glued to their mother's side, watching me closely. *Geez.*

I leaned over the patient and called her name out softly several times before she opened her eyes and stared at me somewhat blankly. "I'm Patti, a nurse from Hospice. I'd just like to look you over so I can help you." She didn't seem to mind as I pulled down her covers to reveal her chest and arms. Ed and Marcie leaned over me as I sat on the edge of the bed and put my stethoscope to my ears. *Geez, Louise,* as my grandfather used to say.

Her pulse and blood pressure were amazingly good. She didn't talk to me, but she followed me with her eyes and responded to my touch. The biggest problems were that she was sleepy, her mouth and skin looked very dry, and her abdomen was distended, like a big balloon filled with water.

I turned toward Ed and Marcie. "I think your mother's kidneys are working. I'd like to insert a catheter and drain the bladder." They stared at me. "It will make her much more comfortable," I added, hopefully.

"No," Marcie emphasized with a slightly louder tone than she had been using. "We don't want any invasive measures. We want her left alone so she can die in peace."

I pulled the covers up over "Mama" and then asked Ed and Marcie to return to the kitchen with me. Ed turned off the bed side light as we left the room. I could see the back yard through the sliding doors. The other adult members of the family were sitting quietly in the shade, and the children were swinging on a play set.

I looked at the children a few minutes to gather strength, and then turned my gaze directly towards Ed and then at Marcie, and said, "I'm very concerned about your mother. But I don't think that she is close to dying. Her blood pressure and pulse are strong. I think she is dehydrated and sedated and her bladder is distended, but she is not close to dying at this time." I could feel my heart thump wildly.

They both glared back at me and were quiet. I heard the children laughing outside. Finally Marcie blurted out, "You haven't been here, you don't know how it has been, she is dying and we are going to make it as easy for her as we can."

Ed turned his back on me as he opened the sliding door to the back yard. "We'd like you to leave now. There is no point in getting us upset."

"And get us something to help her rest, if you want to be helpful," Marcie said angrily as I walked outside clutching my black nurse's bag. I smiled sadly at the children in the yard as Marcie yelled to them to "quit playing at a time like this and get inside."

*　　*　　*

"Are you telling me, Patti, that you think Dr. Wood is mishandling this case?" My head nurse sneered at me behind her large metal desk. She was about my age, thirty-ish, with large erratic black curls that stuck out from her head, and she shouldn't have seemed nearly as intimidating as she did.

"Well, I hate to use those words but I do think there is something weird going on here."

"Well, it sounds to me like you just were not assertive." Before I could respond with an assertive response she added, "You have a tendency to be passive, you know, Patti." I'll call Dr. Wood and see if he will go to visit with you tomorrow to give you some guidelines."

"Thank you," I mumbled, as I got up to leave her office.

*　　*　　*

"We need to put in a catheter, her bladder is distended," demanded Dr. Wood, as he looked from me to Marcie to Ed. He was standing over his patient, having just examined her.

"If that is what you think best," said Marcie with Ed nodding behind her.

I wonder why I didn't think of that. Good thing the doc is here to give me guidelines.

I just happened to have the equipment that I needed for the procedure with me, too. *Ha*

Marcie suggested that she get the doctor some lemonade and so all three of them filed out to the hall to leave me alone with the patient. The other family members had all gone upstairs when Dr. Wood and I arrived, possibly to take late afternoon naps.

"Mama" wasn't talking but she looked straight in my eyes and nodded when I told her that I was going to put a catheter in her bladder. She was cooperative too, while I positioned her legs apart and inserted the small tube in her urethra. Dark yellow urine immediately started to flow, so much so, that I had to clamp the tube several times and wait awhile so she wouldn't lose too much fluid too quickly. I could hear Dr. Wood laughing in the kitchen. He didn't seem to be in any hurry to leave and never did come check on my progress until I had emptied the bag attached to the catheter in the hall toilet three times.

Patricia Taylor

"Dr. Wood, she had three quarts in her," I said as simply as I could, while intentionally not looking at Ed and Marcie, afraid I might yell, 'I told you so!'

"Well that's good it's out. She's probably dehydrated. Let's start giving her fluids, get her bowels moving, and start changing her position in bed. It looks like she's doing better than we had originally thought."

No doubt.

Ed and Marcie looked at him thoughtfully, obviously judging from what the doctor had said that their mother might not be dying right away. They were very quiet while they walked Dr. Wood to the door and then came back to me. They nodded while I made some suggestions as to how to proceed, and then went back to the kitchen while I positioned their mother on her side for the first time in days, and rubbed her wrinkled, red back. It was a miracle she didn't have bed sores.

When I went to the kitchen to tell them that I was finished, they were making a grocery list of juices that they were going to buy for their mother. They started to tell me what schedule they had devised for positioning Mama, and how they would take turns staying with her and talking to her, to stimulate her.

* * *

The next week "Mama" was sitting up in bed with a bright pink bed jacket wrapped around her shoulders, and her hair washed and combed. She looked alert and hydrated, and smiled at me. Marcie explained to her that I was her "wonderful" nurse. "Mama" didn't give any indication of remembering me but she seemed to know Marcie and Ed, and to be comfortable in their house.

Ed worked on his computer in the kitchen and Marcie busied herself with straightening up the living room around us, while I assessed their mother. The curtains were open, and there were no other family members around, so apparently the girls were at school. I removed "Mama's" catheter and helped Marcie to get her mother-in law to a new potty chair next to the bed. Our patient was weak but able to do most of the work with encouragement. Later in the day I called Marcie and she said, "Mama is urinating on her own without any problems."

*   *   *

Two weeks later, "Mama" was sitting up in a chair, fully dressed in colorful pants, shirt and tennis shoes. She looked like she had had her hair permed too. The king sized bed was no longer there. Ed was not home, but Marcie was busy helping her mother-in law eat a tuna sandwich and an orange, with a glass of milk, and talking to her about what "the girls are learning in school." "Mama" nodded while Marcie spoke and still didn't remember me, but she seemed to enjoy her lunch.

After lunch, Marcie turned on the T.V. to *All My Children*, told "Mama" to pay attention to the story, she would be quizzed on it, and asked me to follow her outside. We sat on the patio furniture in the shade and Marcie talked excitedly. "I am calling all the rehabilitation places in town, trying to decide which would be best for Mama. The university has a new experimental program for Alzheimer's. I'm trying to get her into that. Do you know anyone over there? They would keep her all day, and they have a wonderful program that would really keep Mama busy and help her regain some cognitive function, but, if she can't get in right away there are some other half day programs that are good, do you know about any of them?. . . I've been doing lots of research so I know what to expect." *Really? This is so bizarre.*

I listened for about fifteen minutes, not answering any questions. Finally, I blurted out, "You are doing such a good job, and your mom has progressed so much. I don't think you need us anymore." I had been a little afraid to suggest it, but I knew Medicare wouldn't pay for any more visits to a woman who was getting healthier every moment.

I didn't need to fear an angry response.

"Well, we will miss you, but you are right, we are doing fine, but let me know if you hear anything about any of these programs, I think Mama can be cured of this if we just get her into the right program, Ed and I've done some research and there is a lot of new work in Alzheimer's, we just need to find someone with the latest knowledge in this field, do you have any connections at the university?. . ."

I pretty much tiptoed out. And blew a kiss to Mama.

I'll Fly Away

January

I sit on the end of her hospital bed and lie my upper body down by my mother. I stay very still and try to memorize everything about the moment. The door to her hospital room shuts out all the noise and light of the corridor. It is dark in the room except for a sliver of moon shining through the cracked curtain. I feel her hot hand on my forehead and my messy tears over the rest of my face. I taste salt and smell strong surgical soap. I can hear her rhythmic breaths and light snore. After what seemed like ages of trying to ease her surgical pain, she is finally sleeping. But I can't sleep. I have too many thoughts to review in my head and too many fearful feelings squeezing my heart.

Only eight hours ago I was nonchalantly cutting up carrots for the stew my husband and I were preparing for supper. We were in a different part of the country from my mother, not thinking about her at all. I had grabbed the ringing phone and set it on my shoulder while continuing to dice. It was my Dad saying, "Patti you need to sit down."

"What?" I stopped slicing and held very still. I didn't sit down.

"It's Mother. She had a CAT scan today for some back pain. She went for a checkup last week. They thought it was gall bladder but when they did the workup they found out it's her colon. It's cancer and it's already spread to her liver. She's going to surgery in a few minutes to get what they can."

"Oh my God!" I wailed. I was surprised to find that even I said things like this in a crisis. My husband looked at me in alarm and

I grabbed a napkin and pen to write out, *Mother has CANCER!*

"Patti, are you there?" my dad asked anxiously.

"Yes, I'm telling T.J. Where is she?"

From then on I had been in my efficient nurse mode, barely feeling anything. I told my dad I would be there, called my boss and told her I wouldn't be back that week, and packed while my husband arranged the airline flight and lined up a dog sitter. We drove two hours to get to the airport and then flew for an hour and a half. I called to ask how Mother was doing every time I saw a pay phone. And I had rushed to the hospital to find her all alone and in terrible pain; Dad had left thinking she would be in good hands with the nurses. But I had had to fight with them to make sure she got the pain medication she needed and then for help to re-position her to prevent complications after surgery

Finally now that I know she is all right for the moment and comfortable, I can start to feel again. And it hurts. I know what 'colon cancer spread to the liver' means. It means I am going to lose her.

April

"Your tests have come back showing that the chemotherapy is working," Dr. Wright says quietly and calmly. She is a tall brunette with large navy blue glasses that really bring out the blue in her eyes.

My Mother beams and puts her hands together as if in prayer. "I know I am being healed by the Lord."

Dr. Wright smiles weakly but does not respond. She puts the manila folder that contained all the information about mother on a small desk and pulls a black stethoscope out of her pocket. My mother and I are in one of the doctor's examining rooms and she is seeing Dr. Wright before she has her chemotherapy in another area of the clinic.

I sit in a chair by the examining table and watch the assessment.

Mother told me this morning that she always wears the same outfit, 'my chemo dress,' she called it. She said she associates it with a bad day and doesn't want to do that with any of her other clothes. I wonder if she plans to just burn it someday. It's a light blue button up casual dress with yellow flowers. Her head is covered with a yellow turban and she wears pretty navy sandals. And she looks good really. Only the turban gives away her status as a 'chemo patient.' She has lost some weight since she started her treatment, but it makes her look slender rather than too thin. Her color is a healthy pink, not the yellow associated with liver disease. Her brilliant smile completes a picture of someone who is doing very well. This is the first time I have seen her since she has started her treatments, and I am relieved that she is doing so well.

But I know there is a reason why Dr. Wright didn't show more enthusiasm about the tests or Mother's declaration of being healed. She knows the prognosis for metastatic colon disease. I read that there was a less than 30% chance that she would live 5 years. Dr. Wright had already told her and Dad when she started the treatment that the chemotherapy would probably only keep her alive for 2 years. Yet I think now, 30% is not 0%, and if other people could be healed, why not *my* mother? Certainly no one had more confident hope that it was happening than she did.

After the treatment she doesn't look or feel so well. She is drowsy and hangs to her emesis basin like her life depends on it. I take her home. She says the next 24 hours will consist of lots of sleeping but also nausea and occasional sudden vomiting that will exhaust her and make her afraid to take anything by mouth. But then she will feel well again, and continue with her church activities, decorating her new home, and enjoying grandchildren until her next treatment. I will go back to my own life feeling confident for her success.

Patricia Taylor

June

"Mother, how do you feel?" This is our weekly Sunday night phone conversation, and it always starts this way since she's been sick. Before the diagnosis, I never asked that question. If fact, I don't think it ever really occurred to me that she wouldn't always be well before that dreadful night in January.

"Just fine." There is a pause in my mother's refined voice. "Well, maybe a little more tired. It seems to take me longer to recover after my treatments."

This is not like her. Usually she denies any problems. But last week she had briefly mentioned having some hip pain and now she is admitting to being tired. I don't think I have heard her admit to being tired ever before.

"That must be frustrating for you." I can always revert to therapeutic communication when not sure what else to say.

"Yes, it is. I have so much I need to do. We have new volunteer counselors to train and I'm trying to get that women's retreat planned." She is always busy with church activities; those activities, her family, and home are what give her life meaning.

"How is your hip?"

"Well, I can't say it is any better. It might be a little worse." I know for her to say this she must be hurting like hell.

"Did you call Dr. Wright?" I can feel myself getting tense and holding the phone too close to my ear.

"Yes. She said that colon cancer doesn't spread to the bones, so I don't need to worry. I'm thinking it must be arthritis." I wonder why her doctor doesn't plan a bone scan just to be sure.

"Can't you go to someone else for another opinion?"

"Oh, no. Insurance won't pay unless my primary doctor thinks I need to go to someone else. And he's not worried about it."

"Mother, you need to see someone."

"Well, really it's not that bad. I can just take some Ibuprofen and it will be fine. I shouldn't have mentioned it." And just like that I let it go. I want to believe her and I certainly don't know how to push her beyond where she is willing to go.

August

I am crying loudly and uncontrollably as I have done all day on and off. Mother's hip pain is no longer arthritis, but now bone cancer. She has finally had a bone scan and Dr. Wright called this morning to tell her the news and to refer her to another doctor for pain control. I've been with her for a short visit but am scheduled to leave tomorrow.

"I want to stay and take you to your first appointment with the radiologist next week," I shout out between sobs.

Mother leans towards me and takes my hand. "There is no reason for that. Dad can take me just like he does for chemo."

"I know he can. But I want to be here with you." I grab tissues from the box on the table beside the couch where we sit and wipe my face and blow my nose.

"No, you need to go home and take care of T.J. and get back to work."

"But . . ." I start to wail again, and I grab her to me feeling like I can't stand to let her go. She pats my back.

She doesn't seem daunted by the news that the cancer is now in the bone. In fact, she seems relieved that she has a name for the problem and some medication that is actually easing the pain some. And she seems to welcome the radiation, even though it is will just be palliative, as a way to stop the cancer just like she is sure the chemotherapy is doing. She still looks good, though maybe a little too thin and she wears a blond wavy wig that makes her look older; she used to have a straight frosted pixie cut that made her look really cute at the age of 62.

"You need to pray about this and have faith that good will come from this. You are letting the devil get to you," she says pretty firmly when I finally let her go.

I wish she could just sob along with me, and we could curse God and our fates together. I feel like a crazy, bad person for my reaction when she is being so calm and faithful. But she isn't about to start sobbing or cursing so I nod and don't say any more about my staying. I wipe my face again and vow not to cry in front of her any more today.

I'm on my way home and I realize that in her mind any show of negative emotions would be too close for her to giving up. She believes she will be healed and it is important for her to be patient. Also it occurs to me that none of this, her cancer, the spread to the pelvis, then the spread to the bone, was detected earlier because of her refusal to complain. She waited too long to go for tests and then when she did, her extreme efforts not to complain blocked the doctor's ability to see what was going on. I never pushed her to get more help because I always believed things weren't that bad too. I feel crazy again with my impotence in the face of her forced optimism and faith.

September

She isn't looking good any more. My mother lies in her big king sized bed that she shares with my father and my first thought is, 'She looks like a terminal cancer patient.' The few strands of hair that cover her bald head are a murky gray-blond. Her green eyes look enormous in her gaunt face and her body looks small enough to be a child's. She smiles up at me but it isn't her usual brilliant smile; it is

I'll Fly Away   119

almost a grimace and I suspect she is in pain.

"Mother I'm here." I lean over to give her a kiss on the cheek.

"Oh, I'm so glad. How long can you stay?" She holds out her arms to hug my shoulders.

"As long as you need me. I took a leave from work."

"Oh, don't do that. You need to save your time off. I want you to be able to come later, for the holidays." She was doing it again. She was refusing to accept what was clear to everyone else; she was dying.

I took that leave and rushed to her when Dad called to tell me that her latest CAT scan had shown that the chemotherapy was not working and the cancer had spread further into her pelvis. I am determined to stay with her this time until her death even if I can't tell her this now.

"Well, we'll see. For now I'm here with you," I say, putting my lips to her dry cheek again.

Still September

"Mother, how do you feel about the chemotherapy?" I lean anxiously towards her. I have rehearsed this tactic so many times in my head, and I'm still afraid I will get it wrong.

"What do you mean?" She looks at me quizzically and almost skeptically, as if to say, Isn't it obvious how I feel about it? She is leaning back, exhausted, into the large soft brightly colored pillows that cover her favorite white wicker sofa. Her face is white and sunken. She's been up most of the night with waves of nausea that were followed by cramping diarrhea, and unremitting pelvic and leg pain. She is finally having a few moments of respite after several large doses of Imodium and some additional narcotic pills.

"I mean . . . what does Doctor Wright say about how the chemotherapy is working?" I hold my hands tightly together, forcing myself to go slow and not be too pushy about my own opinion about what was going on.

"She says it isn't stopping the cancer from growing. I guess it's just slowing it down some." She smiles weakly still wondering, it seems, what I'm getting at.

"Has she given you any kind of time?" We hadn't ever talked about her death, as she had been so sure she would be healed. And I had wanted to believe it too. But I think now that her denial of the spreading illness is no longer helping her.

"No, she hasn't said anything, but I'll be here for Christmas. In fact, we need to start doing some shopping. I was hoping you could help me with that."

"Yes, of course, Mother, I'll do whatever you want."

She dozes for a few minutes, and I sit back in my chair, taking a deep breath. The room is really a porch off the main living area of my parent's large Victorian home. It is enclosed with glass windows from ceiling to half way down the wall on all sides. They are open at the top and a breeze mingles with a constant row of ceiling fans in the room. It makes the room seem like spring even on this hot Florida morning. Green plants cover the room, sitting on floors interspersed between white wicker chairs and on wicker and glass tables. Bright pink and yellow pillows cover all seated areas. Mother is wrapped in one of her favorite quilts, the one covered with wedding rings in all possible shades of pastels.

The fact that she said she thought she'd still be here for Christmas indicates to me that she knows now she will die from this disease. This gives me hope to push the conversation. I want her here with us for Christmas too and Dr. Wright had given her two years. But now I feel furious for the false hope; I can see that a year was not realistic. It's only been eight months and she no longer has any quality of life. It is consumed with pain from the cancer and then nausea, vomiting and diarrhea from the treatment. I had spent my first day with her taking her to the clinic for her treatment and it and the whole two days and nights since had been a nightmare. She wouldn't be resting now if I hadn't overdosed her on everything I could find in her medicine cabinet. When I had called Dr. Wright she had not given me any help, but said these were normal side effects. Hence, I am on a battle to make things right for my mother, if I can. I've already talked to Dad and the rest of the family and they said they would agree to whatever Mother wants. I just need to know what she wants.

When she wakes up, I start again, "Mother, what would it be like if you didn't take chemo anymore?"

She looks surprised, like she hadn't thought of this before. "I. . ." She stops, staring into space for a long time. But then I know she is really thinking about it because she smiles. It is the first real smile I've seen since my arrival.

"What would it be like?" I say, leaning forward again.

"I wouldn't have to go to the clinic anymore, and I wouldn't be sick. I could just rest here." She closes her eyes and smiles again.

I'm nervous, but I know she needs to think about all the consequences, so I just say it: "What if you don't make it to Christmas?"

She answers right away, without any hesitation. "I'd be in Heaven and with my mother for Christmas."

So that is what she wants. And I can give her that. And not only that, I can do my best to make sure she had a happy pain free time until she dies.

October

I'll Fly Away Oh Glory
I'll Fly Away
By and By Hallelujah By and By
I'll Fly Away

The C.D. player belts out *I'll Fly Away*, as Mother and I sing along. On her first visit the Hospice nurse had brought a Fentanyl patch, a heavy duty long acting narcotic, and within 24 hours it had weaved its way into my mother's blood steam and brain cells and she was transferred into another person I hardly recognize. She laughs and acts silly and sings songs. And, with no chemotherapy and no push from anyone to eat, she no longer has any intestinal problems.

We've been through all the old spirituals several times, and we always come back to this one, *I'll fly Away.*

She is propped up on her wicker sofa, in the same spot she's lived for the last month of her life, with writing paper and pen. She starts to write while still singing and I know it is a letter to one of us: she plans to write a letter to each of her five children for us to read after her death. She has already dictated a list of who is to have each of her belongings after her death, has spoken into a tape recorder about the best memories in her life, and has identified relatives from boxes of old photographs.

I lie on another sofa near her, still singing softly but hoping to doze off a few minutes. I am exhausted from my constant vigil, but happy too.

November

I wear hot pink to her funeral. We follow the program that she designed with her minister before her death, and sing all the old spirituals, including *I'll Fly Away*. I'm high on the idea of her being in heaven with her mother. I know someday I'll join them there. *Hallelujah, I'll Fly Away* too.

December

I'm wearing black now all the time. All my anxiety to have her accept her illness and then to make her last days happy is over. There is nothing left but the realization that she really did fly away. She may be with her mother, but I'm no longer with mine.

Angels Came Down

"*W*e have been redeemed. Some cherubs found us and realized that we had been left behind," Jerry says as he looks earnestly into my face.

"Uh huh," I respond, nodding encouragement and meeting his eyes. He looks ahead and is quiet for a few minutes, apparently satisfied that I have heard and understand. We are walking a tree-lined path that leads to the recreation area of the old state mental hospital. Green leaves are starting to appear and flowers are budding. It's cool, sweater weather, and sunny, and it feels great to be outside after the cold, wet winter. It doesn't get really cold in Alabama like it does other places but it still feels pretty miserable to us just the same. Jerry and I both watch as a cardinal flits in a tree.

"My mother was told that if she had me she would die," Jerry suddenly pronounces.

"That must've been awful for her." I give him what I hope is a sad, concerned look.

"It was. I am alive but her spirit was split into pieces and she is everywhere. I feel her around me all the time." He smiles as he motions with his hands and arms to indicate her presence around his head and body. I'm happy for him that this seems to be a peaceful delusion. In the past I've known him to be agitated and fearful, needing to be restricted to his unit because of his idea that the devil was manifesting himself in other people.

We enter the courtyard to the recreation area and join several people, some dressed oddly, standing alone or in groups, or sitting on benches at picnic tables. It is early, the patients have just begun to fill this popular area, and they all are smoking cigarettes. Some hold sodas from a nearby machine. The only patients in conversation are two who are sitting by nursing students, and they seem to be enjoying the extra attention. One young woman holds a small pink radio from which rock music blares. No one moves to the music, but no one seems to be bothered by it either.

I say *Hello* as we approach the group and everyone nods or returns the greeting. They know that I am the nursing students' instructor; they have seen me here every week for the last two months and some have seen me every winter in this capacity for many years.

Jerry immediately pulls a cigarette from his pocket and asks Bob, a young man sitting on a bench with a student, for a light. Bob holds his cigarette out and Jerry lights his cigarette from Bob's. This is one way that I've noticed that the patients take care of each other. They don't have lighters at their disposal but they manage to keep each other's smokes going all day. I guess a staff member starts the first one in the morning. I've also noticed a lot of sharing of cokes and snacks, cigarettes, and small change.

We sit down beside Bob and his student nurse, Ben. Bob is a handsome man of about thirty with sparkling dark eyes. He wears jeans that are too big for him, without a belt, and two pullover sweaters that seem too tight; the top is red and the one sticking out from under is purple. He wears a large yellow comb stuck into the top of his short stiff black hair. He occasionally takes it out and sweeps over his head with comb and hand, like an Elvis impersonator. We all sit without talking. For several minutes Bob looks at us and laughs aloud, a Ha-Ha-Ha laugh, and Ben and I smile back nervously. We aren't sure what he is going to come out with. Jerry and the other patients often ignore Bob. In the past Jerry has called Bob 'crazy.'

Suddenly Bob yells at me, "Willie, you caught up with me."

I nod. He turns to Ben, pointing at me, "I know her, she is my wife," then jumps up and points at another patient on the other side of the courtyard, "That man over there. That man owes me fifteen thousand dollars. I'm her pimp." He laughs again, Ha- Ha-Ha, and pulls at his jeans that have fallen below his navel. Ben and I laugh too. Bob is always outrageous in his beliefs and comments. For that reason he is normally not allowed outside his unit without supervision. We are happy that the staff let us bring him here today. Ben asks him to sit down and, as Bob does so, Ben tries to distract him by starting another conversation. I turn to Jerry.

"Is this your last day?" Jerry asks, grabbing my hand.

"Yes, I'm sorry. I'll miss you." And I really am sorry; I always hate it when the end of our rotation comes, and I know I won't be back for another ten months.

"Will you take me home with you?" he asks, as he has asked every day that I've spent with him.

"That would be nice if I could, wouldn't it," I reply as I have every day that I've spent with him. I smile and squeeze his hand.

"I have been discharged. I can go anywhere I want to." I nod, knowing it's best not to argue. "I've been kept here prisoner but I've served my time. Angels came down and said 'Jerry White, you can go free.'"

I smile and nod again. There is absolutely nothing to say to this that would be helpful. We sit quietly for awhile. The rock music continues to blare from the pink radio. We've been able to talk, but it would be so much more peaceful without it. Still, I think that it helps to calm the inner voices for a lot of the patients, so it works that way.

While we sit and listen to Bob talk excitedly to Ben over the din of the radio, I feel again my rising frustration that Jerry and lot of people like him are doomed to serve a prison-like sentence for the rest of their lives because they have brain disorders like schizophrenia, bipolar disease, and severe clinical depression.

In institutions, most people are admitted for acute exacerbations of their illness, are stabilized on medication, and then sent out into the community within a short time. Most live in the community in some fashion, ideally with family, group homes, or individual apartments. But we do not have adequate community resources anywhere in our country, and a lot of patients spend more time in jail or on the streets than anywhere else.

For people like Jerry who don't respond to medicines at all and are a danger to themselves or others, this hospital is their home for a great deal of their lives. It is awful for the students to realize this, but I say that at least these patients have a safe environment, shelter and food.

I'm interrupted from my reverie by Bob. He jumps up and down while he shouts, "I'm a white Canadian Egyptian pharaoh!" He pulls at his pants that are falling again while he hops around the picnic table. "They dipped me in shit to make me black and that's why I'm a warrior." He laughs his strange laugh, and Ben tells Bob to quiet down. Ben knows that Bob won't be allowed to come out with us if he gets too disruptive.

Jerry ignores Bob and asks me if I'll buy him a cup of coffee. I slip him fifty cents. We aren't supposed to buy things for the patients, but I figure they have so few pleasures that a little spoiling won't hurt.

Later that morning, ten nursing students meet me at the entrance to the women's chronic ward. It is blocked by a large gray locked metal door. The hall to the unit is painted a dull white with no relief from pictures, murals, or plants. Paint is peeling around the top of the door. I knock and stand on tiptoes to see through the small unbreakable window. Finally, a staff member sees me and slowly heads towards the door with her keys in tow. When she opens the door, we all enter as a group carrying a cooler of cokes and ice, bags of chips, cookies, and paper plates and cups.

About fifteen women patients crowd around us; there are too many to count or to really talk with individually. They all speak to us at once, and touch us, and ask what we have brought them. I recognize most of these women from each year that I've visited; they are like Jerry in that they have no place else to go. Most of them are so unstable that they are not allowed to walk the grounds with the students. So we have brought a party to them.

While we head to a small closed off room with table and chairs to set up the snacks, the three staff members dressed in pink scrubs yell at the patients not to get too close to us. They are not nurses; in fact I never see nurses on the unit with the patients. The nurses sit on the other side of the locked door in the nurses' station with their charts. The staff members with us are unlicensed personnel and are responsible for direct around the-clock-supervision of the patients. A staff member yells again, and the women hold back and let the students pass into the room furnished with tables and benches.

As the students set up the goodies, I stay outside with the patients. Chairs and small couches too heavy to lift are arranged in long rows that face a television behind a heavy bolted piece of plastic. The staff settles to watch a daytime soap opera, and the patients clamor around me again.

Julie, a blond petite woman who looks like she should still be on the adolescent unit, tells me she is Snow White and Grace Kelly. "I have a mansion in Beverly Hills filled with gold and silver. I'll give it to you if you get me out of here," she says. Shonna, a large black woman, over six feet tall, with scars across her forehead and cheek, laughs and tells me not to pay any attention to Julie. Julie starts to cry and I put my arm around her and she stops crying. Bobbie, with dyed blond hair and dark black roots, wears Big Bird slippers and calls me *Mama*. Shonna tells Bobbie that I am not her mother and Bobbie cries. I pat her on the hand, as Maggie, who wears a baseball cap and jeans asks if we can play cards and can she lead the Hokey Pokey.

Shonna says she wants to sing for us. Cheryl, who is sixty-something, gets close enough to tell me that she birthed thirty- three babies last night and just found out she is pregnant again. Shonna laughs and calls Cheryl *crazy*. Mona, a heavy-set woman in a purple nightgown, laughs at Cheryl too and then tells me she herself is not sick like everyone else here, but is a secret undercover agent for the CIA, and asks if I can get a message to them.

I see Karen across the room sitting near a staff member. She wears a motorcycle-like helmet to prevent her from hurting her head when she bangs it against a wall. Now she rocks back and forth. I catch her eye and wave and she waves back, but does not get up to approach me until the students announce that the refreshments are ready.

Twenty women, everyone on the unit except one woman who has slept cramped on a too small couch since we entered, finds a place at one of the picnic tables in the room. They eat and drink everything set in front of them and then keep all ten students and me busy with their requests for more: "More coke, please, more Cheetos. Are there more cookies? Did you bring candy?"

Shonna sings "Amazing Grace" in a deep throaty voice and we all clap. Several women tell dirty jokes and all the patients laugh uproariously while the students and I roll our eyes. Bobbie keeps yelling out *Mama* at me and Shonna and Maggie tell her to shut up.

Patricia Taylor

Sue, a young black woman who never speaks at all, starts to sing "You light up my life." Suddenly the room is quiet except for her beautiful perfect voice; for a few minutes everyone looks at peace. Then Bobbie starts to sing along with her and several of the woman and students join in, all sounding terribly out of tune, but joyous.

The party ends with the Hokey Pokey, led by Maggie, and we all put our butts in and shake them all around. As the students clean up, I play a game of Spades with Maggie. Others hover over me and continue to talk, while Maggie yells at them to leave us alone. She wins the game with her own special rules.

The students and I finally say our goodbyes and Bobbie clings to me yelling *Mama,* and is pulled away and held comfortingly by Shonna.

The students leave the facility to go out to lunch. I sit in my car, too tired to go anywhere or to talk to anyone for an hour.

I've finished lunch and am waiting for Jerry outside the recreation hall. We agreed earlier to meet here so we can go to the record hop together. This is the most popular event of the week and patients are streaming towards the ear-splitting recreation hall from all directions.

Bob and Ben show up. Bob says he wants a cigarette before he goes into the dance, so he gets a light from another patient and they stand with me. Bob is very quiet for a few minutes, cocking his head and smiling at no one in particular. Ben and I eye each other. Suddenly Bob yells, "I went up there and there were vampires and wolves." He starts to dance around with his arms out in front of him like he is boxing, while his pants fall down. "They were fighting and baring their teeth." Bob grins at us viciously. "There were red vampires and white wolves. I'm not going there no more." He shakes his head back and forth emphatically."

Ben asks, "Where?"

"In the sky!" Bob answers indignantly and glares at Ben, as he crushes his cigarette under his foot.

"Oh," says Ben and looks at me sheepishly.

"Bob, are you ready to go inside," I ask.

Bob is quiet and looks like he is starting to turn and walk in the direction of the music when he abruptly stops and points to another patient. He pronounces, "That man is thirty-five million years old. He doesn't have to worry about money. He doesn't answer to anyone."

Ben starts to walk, encouraging Bob to follow him, but Bob continues talking to another patient. "You owe me sixty thousand billion dollars for her." He points at me. Ben takes Bob by the arm and tells him it is time to leave.

Bob follows passively, saying to me, "Goodbye sweetheart." Luckily the other patient has totally ignored Bob; he sits staring into space.

I sit on a bench beside Luther. Luther never talks unless spoken to and sits with his head in his hands, his forehead creased. Luther has always refused to spend time with a student because he says he has things to work out. And he doesn't go to dances either. Normally, I can barely follow him. His speech is always so rushed and pressured.

"I'm waiting for the canteen worker, Peggy, to get back from lunch, she's my best friend, I'm gonna make her a pillow, a yellow one with blue trim, I've been invited to the white house, I can't get hold of them, I need someone to take me up there, I contacted the secret service and hope they'll help me, I've got to get out of here, I need someone to know that I'm pregnant, it's twins, I'm worried how they'll get out, I need an ultrasound, they'll have to go out my bladder and that will hurt, can you help me?"

"You sound like you are having a really bad day," I say inanely. Of course, being a male, pregnant with twins, and needing to get out of here and to the white house, with no one to help you would be worse than having a bad day.

"I am. I need to be left alone to work this out." Luther bows his head again and I leave him alone.

Jerry shows up saying he overslept at nap time. He grabs my hand as we head towards the dance. The patients are not allowed to touch us, or anyone else for that matter, but I believe that they need the feel of another human body; isn't that a basic human need for all of us?

We slow dance and I let him hold me just a little closer than I should. He is a big muscular man with a mustache and beard. He looks and feels great in his leather jacket, jeans and cowboy boots.

"Will you take me home with you?"

"That would be nice wouldn't it?"

"I've been kept prisoner, but I've served my time. The angels came down and redeemed us and set me free."

I'm exhausted; I've danced every dance. But the music has finally stopped and it's time for us to go home. Students and patients alike lined up to do the Macarena and the Electric Slide that have recently become popular. I danced on the periphery with patients like me who can't follow the line dances. We held hands and swayed or twirled each other around. I know the students think I'm corny and that's O.K.

The patients crowd around us all asking for goodbye hugs

which we freely give, despite disapproving glances from the staff. Jerry waits till last and gives me an especially long close hug. I tell him I'll see him next time I bring students.

I head back to my life with no locked doors, with a job and an affectionate family and friends and a car and cokes and cigarettes and cookies any time I want them. On the way home I think about Jerry and Bob and Julie and Shonna and Maggie and Cheryl and Mona and Karen and Sue and Luther. I pray that the angels will come down and realize who has been left behind.

Patricia Taylor

The Quality Nurse

"*W*hy is 202 still here?" Ms. Cassandra throws her census sheet on the table and sighs heavily. She does this or some variant of it every day, so I know not to literally answer her question, or even react in any way.

Why are you still here?

She's been asking me questions about my patients for the last thirty minutes. I actually have work to do.

We are in the nursing station, which is a dark room smaller than a lot of people's walk in closets. In the center is a round table and on it sits a circular rack of medical records where she is sitting and examining charts. She's wearing a bright, colorful blouse that clashes with her red, obviously dyed, hair that she has pinned up in a loose bun. Every day she smells like something you could eat; today it is coconut.

"She's used up all of her Medicaid days three days ago," Ms Cassandra says, in her condescending tone. "She needs to go home with home health. Why aren't you doing any discharge planning?" I still don't answer, and I guess she doesn't expect me to because she's bent over, writing something.

"202" is Mrs. Hope, a thirty- year- old woman who has un-controlled diabetes and a urinary tract infection that she can't get over.

"They just started her on another antibiotic last night when her temp spiked to 102 again," I volunteer. "She can't possibly leave now."

"Good grief." She nods her head and sighs.

Ms Cassandra is our QUALITY CONTROL nurse, an RN who monitors what kind of care patients get and how long they stay in the hospital. She gets details about the patient' status from the medical record and nurse reports and then she gives the physicians her recommendations. It's a mandatory position because of Medicare laws.

She explained her role to me in the first week of my orientation when I started working here six months ago. So, I know someone has to do it, but still. She says it's about good and cost efficient medical care, but I think all she cares about is making sure the hospital doesn't lose any money. We call her **Miss** Cassandra because she is like, in her seventies or something, and has been doing this forever. I'm not sure she ever did any real nursing though.

When she has asked her 100 questions and reviewed all eight medical records, Ms Cassandra marches off toward the doctor's lounge in her high heels and too short skirt to give Dr Crum her recommendations. She never takes the time to visit any patients, so she has no clue what's really going on, outside of her cushy office.

This is a really small rural hospital and our in-patient census is usually around ten. But we have a hopping ER and frequent admissions. Also I'm expected to run over to the ER and help that nurse when they get too busy. I'm just getting back to staff nursing after teaching psychiatric nursing at a university for twenty years and I'm severely out of practice in the real world of medical surgical nursing. I somehow thought the load would be easier than in a big hospital but it's not so.

So by the time Miss Cassandra leaves, I'm totally behind on my own work. I haven't even assessed the patients yet this morning and the doctor will be here soon to make rounds. Luckily, I have an LPN, Joyce, to work with me today who will give the meds and a nursing tech, Mary, who will do vital signs, blood sugars and baths, but as the RN, I'm responsible for everything.

I rush to each room in my sloppy teal scrubs, which I never can make myself iron, my red New Balance shoes, and a pink stethoscope around my neck.

Mrs. Hope is sitting up, supported by the head of the bed, wearing a dingy blue and white hospital gown and covered by a pale blue spread. She smiles weakly, and calls me honey. Sunshine flows through the big windows, which seems to make her smaller and paler than she already is. A clear IV bag is hanging over her right arm and a urine bag is clamped to the side of the bed. The urine is dark, like over-brewed tea, and smells sickening like ammonia only worse.

"Have your bowels moved? Are you in any pain? Have you eaten breakfast?" I reel off all the usual nurse questions and she answers yes or no.

When she says, "No, I haven't eaten," I finally slow down.

"You know you need to eat. You had insulin today, and that will drop your blood sugar too much if you don't eat."

"I know, honey, but I'm just not hungry and I'm too tired to eat," she replies in her soft southern accent. She does look tired and very fragile. "But, I'll try to take some juice and crackers."

I leave her and ask Mary, the nursing tech, to take graham crackers and a glass of orange juice to Mrs. Hope, just as Dr. Crum starts yelling out my name. He literally stands in the hall until I come running with a rolling rack of medical records to follow him to each patient's room.

I explain how the patients have been in the last twenty four hours. We discuss Mrs. Hope's fever and the new antibiotic started last night by the doc on call. I notice the orange juice and crackers sitting on the bedside table, untouched. I think to mention that Mrs. Hope isn't eating, but then I'm rushing after Dr. Crum to the next room and focusing on the next patient.

Later, as I check all the doctor's new orders, I note that he didn't actually take any of Miss Cassandra's recommendations seriously. For instance, Cassandra had said the doc needed to have blood cultures run on Mrs. Hope when her temp goes back up. That was so that the docs would know for sure what kind of infection she had and if it had gone into her blood. It is a Medicare requirement and a good idea, I guess, but the docs just do what they want around here, regardless of quality standards. And no one was discharged either.

When I finally sit down, so that I can document everything regarding all the patients' assessments, it's eleven thirty in the morning, almost lunch time for the patients. I grab a nutty fruity granola bar because I know I'm not going to get any real lunch myself; I never do. The director of nurses insists that I take a break because there are 30 minutes every day that I don't get paid, but she never offers to relieve me so I can't do it. She's off today, anyway.

The phone rings, for the fiftieth time this morning, and I want to scream. *Why isn't the switchboard picking up these calls?* But it is Mary the nursing tech, telling me to come to Mrs. Hope's room right away. I drop my granola bar on the nurse's desk, and rush to room 202.

Mary has the blood sugar monitor in her hand and is shaking the woman.

"Mrs. Hope!" I yell. She's slumped to her right side in the bed. Her skin is ghastly white and she is perspiring. She doesn't respond to either of us.

"Her blood sugar is twenty," Mary says. It should be between eighty and one hundred.

I pick up the bedside phone and dial 400, our emergency line, connected to an intercom that goes out to the whole hospital. I hear my voice over-head as I speak, "Joyce to 202 with D50 immediately and Lab STAT." D50 is an intravenous injection of 50 percent glucose that should bring her blood sugar up quickly. The lab is supposed to draw blood before we give glucose to verify her glucose is low.

I stand on the right side closest to the door while Mary pulls Mrs. Hope's body up straight in the bed. I can feel my chest getting heavy and I'm afraid I'm going to have an asthma attack.

Joyce runs in with the glucose but the lab tech is not with her. After a few seconds, I pull an alcohol pad from my pocket, pick up the IV line, and swab the port closest to Mrs. Hope. For the first time, I notice the IV fluid isn't flowing and when I try to inject the medicine it won't go it. The line is either kinked or clogged off. I spend two seconds looking for a kink but there is none. I finally notice it is clogged off with blood where it goes into her hand. I forgot to check and flush it when I made rounds. *Shit, not now*

I grab the phone again and yell into the intercom system. "Doctor Crum and ER nurse to 202 with code cart." I know there is a med on the emergency cart, Glucagon, which can be given intramuscularly with a doctor order.

Mary pulls the vital sign machine close, wraps the blood pressure cuff around Mrs. Hope's thin left upper arm and hits START. Lights start flashing and end with the blood pressure reading of 80/50. It is too low: dangerously so. Joyce runs to get the IV start tray at my request.

When she returns, I pick an IV catheter and a pre-filled syringe of saline and a tourniquet from the orange tackle box where we keep IV supplies. I apply the tourniquet to her right arm but can't find a vein to even try to stick.

I should have made sure she drank that juice or ate. I should have rechecked her glucose hours ago. I should have kept this damn

IV line open.

The ER nurse doesn't show. My chest is tighter. I can't take a deep breath.

Dr. Crum arrives. Joyce tells him what is going on and he sees me struggling to find a vein. He demands, "Get that IV in."

Yeah, start an IV. Why didn't I think of that?

He doesn't offer to help.

"Joyce, get me a smaller cath," I yell, as I find one small vein in Mrs. Hope's wrist, and then dig around in the unorganized IV tray.

Dr Crum starts cussing. He is standing at the end of the bed with his arms crossed.

I could kill him.

Joyce runs out of the room. I try to stick another site while I tell Dr Crum, "The cart with Glucagon is on the way."

"Well, where is it? Damn it," he demands. Mrs. Hope is not responding at all to the IV sticks or anything else. Her breathing is swallow and she's deathly pale.

The noise of scratchy wheels makes me turn towards the door. Joyce has returned followed by the mobile emergency cart, pushed by Miss Cassandra, of all people.

Miss Cassandra nudges me aside to maneuver the cart close to the bed, pulls the doors of the cart open, and grabs the IV equipment. In seconds, she starts the IV in Mrs. Hope's upper arm on the first try and yells at me to hand her the glucose solution. As she pushes the glucose, Mary checks vital signs again. Her blood pressure, pulse and respiratory rate are all too low. Dr. Crum yells out his orders for the glucose, a heart monitor, other emergency drugs, and IV fluids at the same time that Miss Cassandra is already on it. I follow her orders, standing as close to the top of the bed as I can to get out of Miss Cassandra's way. I hand her things from the cart as she demands, though clumsily.

But then, rather quickly, Mrs. Hope starts to revive. She is moving and her color is improving.

"Mrs. Hope, are you OK?" Miss Cassandra asks.

She opens her eyes and looks at all of us weakly. "What are y'all doing?"

Miss Cassandra, Joyce, Mary and I all laugh with relief, while Mary checks Mrs. Hope's glucose and vital signs. She is stabilizing.

"Let's transfer her," orders Dr Crum, as he leaves the room. I run after him, getting truly short of breath, to make the arrangements to send her to a higher level facility.

I knew Mrs. Hope was too sick to go home today. But darn, Miss Cassandra is a real quality nurse.

Enid, Ward Six

"*H*i, I'm Queen Elizabeth One and I just came back as the new royal heir. Who are you? Do you want to talk to me?"

"Nice to meet you, I'm Patti, the registered nurse tonight," I respond, while shaking the delicate pale hand offered me. "Yes, I'd love to talk to you. I'll come find you later."

She smiles, turns swiftly, walks to the nearest chair, and sits primly with a posture that would make any queen proud.

I continue through the day area, towards the nurses' station, and through a crowd of patients, some with smiles and hugs, some with concern ("I want to know what the doctor said about me.") and some with good news to share ("I'm going home next week.") Others stand or sit quietly with glaring or indifferent stares. Some completely ignore me while sleeping, watching TV or talking, apparently to voices coming from inside their own brains.

I've recently finished orientation at this Alabama state psychiatric hospital. I'm the evening charge nurse and always apprehensive at this point in the day, never knowing what to expect.

The nurses' station is blocked to the patient entrance with two locked doors. I use my keys to go through. The area inside is really just a tiny, hot, crowded room that is covered with old mustard-colored paint. Ward Six's mental health team members sit around an unstable table with mismatched chairs. Medical records cover the table. Everyone is female, although we are a variety of nationalities and races. The psychiatrist is writing new orders while the day shift RN is talking with her about a patient who has been "acting out seductively." The social worker, the recreation leader, and the dietitian are also squeezed around the table, reviewing documents, making their own entries, and commenting on the same patient. Those of us who are here to work the next shift stand in corners and wait for report. All the nursing staff wear brightly colored scrubs that could make us wrongly resemble a happy group of workers. My feet already hurt.

Report entails the day shift RN telling us, the 3-11 shift staff, about what has happened on the ward the last 16 hours. The staff includes me, Selma, the licensed practical nurse who will give all medications, and the five unlicensed mental health techs who are to provide physical care and safety. While we are trying to listen and take notes, everyone at the table is trading medical records and talking at once. We leave report with minimal information on what is going on with the 25 patients we are caring for tonight. Luckily, we are familiar with most of the patients who have been here for a while or of those who we see often and are called "frequent fliers."

I leave the station as soon as possible to get away from the stifling heat and noise of constant chatter, only to encounter more heat and ear-splitting screaming in the day room. Abby, a 30-something obese female, is leaning over the waist- high counter that partitions off an area for the staff. Abby's dull eggplant waist-length hair shields her face, but her hands are gripping the edge of the counter, and I can hear her pleading.

"I need my clothes and my Bible, I was promised them three days ago." She has been calm and cooperative this admission, so I'm guessing she has been asking about this for awhile.

Barbara, a tall muscular mental health tech is sitting inside the enclosed area, taunting back angrily, "Get away from the counter and go sit down, or you won't get to go to the dance." Three other techs chime in with the same advice.

Abby screams "But I need my clothes to wear to the dance, I have a right to my Bible." She pounds on the counter with both fists.

Selma, the LPN who is a skinny woman with a permanent scowl, dashes from the medication room, threatening, "Go sit now or you're going to get a shot," pointing towards chairs in the day area.

Abby sobs, "No, I don't want a shot," hangs her head, turns and plods heavily towards a group of bolted down orange seats.

I start to intervene, and then give up. Once again I realize that no amount of role modeling or teaching of the staff is ever enough to change anything in a positive way. And I know there is no point in asking a tech to get the patient's belongings from the storage area; there will be a reason why it is impossible tonight. I'll have to find the time to get the key from the supervisor and get Abby's stuff myself.

I hear Selma, Barbara, and the others laughing as I head toward Abby and the other patients. The day room is large and dark with no windows and old lime paint covering the walls. There are a few scattered posters taped up with inane messages like, **HANG IN THERE**, and a picture of a cat hanging upside down. Patients sit in several semi-circles. One group has the TV on with *The Price is Right*, and another group has chairs surrounding a table and is playing rummy. Most of the group settings are not groups at all, but individual patients sitting alone.

I listen to Abby's concerns, inform her of my resolve to help and then inquire how she is in other ways. I do this with the entire group of patients in the area, reminding several that I can't talk individually with anyone now or play cards, although this is really all I want to do, spend the evening listening and supporting everyone individually and playing cards. You can learn a lot about people when you play cards with them.

Several patients are in their bedrooms, which are off a hall that smells of harsh chemical with hints of urine. The rooms house two patients per room. Each bedroom contains two beds, small wood chairs and dressers and no personal items except a few clothes and shoes. Shampoos and other hygiene items are kept locked in the day area.

When I enter Enid's room, she is alone, and I'm surprised to find her lying on her bed with a thin white blanket covering her entire body. She is usually sitting up in bed reading this time of day. I touch what appears to be a bony shoulder and call her name. The shroud stirs and I am suddenly looking into her beautiful, intelligent face. She is a tall thin woman, her skin and hair the color of dark cocoa, and she is wearing a forest green sweater that brings out the blue/green in one eye while the other eye stays dark brown. She smells like vanilla extract, a lotion that she has managed to keep with her under the covers.

But she is not smiling like she usually does when I greet her. I note the beginnings of a bruise the size of a 50 cent piece on her left cheek, and she is cradling her left arm against her chest.

"What's the matter, Enid? What happened?" I sit on a chair near the bed and lean towards her.

"I was hit and then pushed into the wall by one of the techs." She points to the wall behind where I am sitting. "All because I refused to take my meds today and they all hate me anyway."

I replied, "You were hit and pushed? Who did it?"

"A tech, on days, I don't know her name. My shoulder is killing me. It feels like it's broken," she says as she grabs her left shoulder with her right hand.

I assess her left shoulder, arm and cheek. She cries out when I touch the areas. There's another larger dark red area on the upper front of her arm. However, I don't think anything is broken. "Did the nurses know? Did you get anything for pain?"

"I told both of them but I didn't get anything."

Even though report was hectic, I'm pretty sure no one mentioned this. And I believe Enid, because she isn't one to fabricate. And she is right; she is not liked by the staff. That is because she has strong opinions on what she needs and has no trouble sharing them with any of us. She has been here two weeks and has refused just about everything that has been offered to her including most of her meds, classes, recreation, and team meetings. She stays in her room alone, usually reading or writing letters. But still . . . there is never, ever, an excuse for abuse.

Back in the nurses' station, I call the medical nurse practitioner and report Enid's injuries. He orders X-Rays and Tylenol for pain. I explain the situation to Barbara and Selma who are sitting at the table, telling them that I'm going to call the hospital's police to start an investigation. I ask Barbara to transport Enid to radiology. They are both glaring at me but are, for once, deathly quiet. I ask, "What is wrong," as I look into their angry faces.

Finally, Selma speaks up. "You shouldn't do this. You might get someone fired. And besides, Enid is just trying to get attention."

What? Someone who abuses a patient shouldn't lose her job? And Enid threw her body into a wall to get attention when all she ever wants is to be left alone? I don't think so.

"Well, it's our legal responsibility to report this. I don't see how I can't follow through. And Selma, please give Enid some Tylenol before she goes." They both look at me like they've never met anyone like me before, not in a good way. I notify the police and my immediate supervisor, and I begin to write out the event on an official Incident Report. Selma and Barbara slowly get up and leave me alone in the station. From outside the doors I hear loud, rapid conversation.

Within a half an hour, Max, a tall, very sexy police officer shows up with his camera and clipboard, smelling of some kind of manly cologne. He is wearing a beige state hospital police uniform with an ominous black holster on his belt. Max smiles and every time he does this, all of us want to follow him home. That is **ONE** thing all the female staff have in common.

He flirts with us, and then interviews Enid alone in her room. He will take pictures of her bruises, I know. And then an investigator will be assigned to collect all relevant information including another interview with Enid and then one with me and other staff that were on duty earlier today.

Now, I'm totally behind on all the things I'm supposed to be doing tonight. However, before I can start anything else, I need to take the Incident Report to Shelly, my nursing supervisor. I unlock and lock several more doors as I rush down a long winding hallway to arrive at her office. I knock and am told to come in.

I enter the room, seeing Shelly behind a large wood desk. The desk is overflowing with piles of paper. There is also a bookcase filled with manuals, and two tall green filing cabinets. They are covered with junk food items, mostly Chocolate chip cookies and Nacho chips, and a six pack of COKE. Neither the walls nor furniture have pictures nor any personal items, except a white lab coat hanging from a hook on the wall behind her. It all smells like dust and mold, just like every other room in the hospital. I sit in the only chair that faces her desk, hugging myself from the cold air coming from a single AC unit behind me. The Incident Report sits on my lap.

Shelly's long red nails tap the top of her desk. Bright yellow hair, obviously newly dyed, sits in a knot on the top of her head with tendrils falling around her puffy, wrinkled sagging neck and forehead. She is pretty in a disillusioned way; she's worked here her entire nursing career, which has been at least 40 years. She's wearing an orange paisley, silky-looking blouse with a big bow around her neck and big gold hoops on each ear. I've never seen her in scrubs or her lab coat.

I smile and ask her how she is. She smiles back, but doesn't answer my question. Instead, she says, "Patti, I'm glad you came down, because I need to talk to you about some things."

Oh, Oh, I'm in trouble again.

"Oh? Well I needed to bring you this report." I push the form towards her.

She takes hold of the report and looks at it awhile with her lips clamped together into a fine line. I am quiet too, and I take the time to examine her desk more carefully. On the desk, between papers and lots of pens, is a cell phone opened to a solitaire game.

Finally, she looks up and points to the report. "This is one of the things I wanted to talk to you about. I see no reason for you to start all this fuss."

"But. . ."

"But nothing. These people need their jobs. Plus, they have been here a lot longer than you have and they know these patients. Enid will do whatever she needs to do to get her own way." She reaches up to massage her stooped shoulders while she continues, "And the staff has complained that you always want to do things your own way. You act like you are in charge."

I couldn't let this go by. I stammered, "But I **am** in charge. I'm the RN and the supervisor. I'm legally responsible for everything that happens on the ward when I'm here."

"I do not need a lecture, what I am saying is that you are part of a team and everyone's needs must be considered. You don't listen to them at all. You interfere with their decisions about the patients. You watch the staff all the time, like you are trying to get them in trouble.

And you actually asked them to sign in and out when they leave the ward."

I'm not sure what to respond to first, and I notice I'm twirling my wedding ring around my finger. "But I'm signing in and out myself, too. It's just so we know where everyone is, especially if there's an emergency. I don't even know when people leave and come back for dinner. And I do have a license I'm trying to protect, and an RN should decide how to handle major patient issues."

My voice has risen into one long whine.

"You're so OCD about everything. I really think psych nursing at this facility is not going to be for you," she replies. Shelley's face is set, as if she just made a big decision.

I'm so wound up that I ignore her expression and keep going. "But I love psych patients. I want to provide a therapeutic, healing environment."

"You should have figured out by now that what you taught in nursing school is not the way it is in real life. These can be very dangerous people and you are setting yourself up to be hurt when you are so friendly," she informs me impatiently.

"But, aren't I more likely to get hurt if I'm mean? Shouldn't being nice and caring help me? And I do pay attention. When there is any sign of hostility, I try to handle the situation as soon as possible."

She ignores me and continues, "You have no idea how to supervise." She sighs and looks down a few moments. "Can you at least admit you started out on the wrong foot with the staff?"

I breathe deeply and lower my voice. "Yes, I admit that I was too bossy at first. I should've gotten to know the culture of this place before starting to really supervise. I wrote those techs up for sleeping on the job. Maybe I should have tried to make some friends while I watched how things work."

Shelley nods her head and for the first time in this interview she looks a little happier.

But I have to go on. "I swear, it never entered my mind that anyone would not take me seriously as a supervisor. Or that is was OK to sleep when watching patients. Or to be physically abusive. I really thought we were all on the same page with hierarchy and patient rights and safety."

Suddenly the 1812 Overture blares from her phone. Shelley picks it up. "I'll call you back in a minute . . . no, I'm not busy." She hangs up. I have my wedding ring off now and about to drop it the way I'm moving it from hand to hand.

She looks back at me and talks, as if I hadn't said that last thing about patient rights. "I'm glad you admit that you have some deficits. We'll talk more about this when we do your three-month evaluation next month."

I nod and put my ring back on my finger. I'm imagining telling my husband that I may not actually have a job much longer. *So long, trip to Utah to see the Shakespeare Festival.*

"Meanwhile," she continues, "You need to re-write this report. It is not written professionally."

OK, let it go. You know you know how to write, but it doesn't matter now. Just try to be polite and keep your job. I replied, "Yes, I'll do that. Can you give me an example of what would sound better?"

When I finally leave her office, with notes scribbled on the edges and back of the report, she smiles her delighted smile like she did when I entered. "Just stay in the nursing station and let the staff do their job. You are not working in a timely manner. Don't talk to the patients unless you need to, but for no more than 5 minutes. Most of these people you probably know enough about you can just write a note on the medical record without actually interviewing them."

Patricia Taylor

I'll let hell freeze over before I stop talking to patients and let the staff do whatever they want. I smile too, as I close the door and lock Shelly into the safety of her personal space.

I practically run back to the ward, remembering that I forgot to ask for the key so I could get Abby's clothes and Bible. I guess that would not have gone over well.

I enter ward six again, I notice that the patients are quieter than usual and all the staff are behind the partitioned area in the day area. They look at me with smug expressions. I rush past them into the nurses' station to rewrite the report. The nurse practitioner calls to say Enid's X-rays are negative.

When I return to Shelly's office with the revised report, she's not there, probably left the hospital to get something to eat, so I gratefully slide the form under her door.

Back on the ward again, Barbara tells me that Enid is refusing to leave her room for dinner. I suggest that I get her to come to the day area and the staff can bring food to her from the cafeteria since she has had a rough day.

Barbara snaps, "If she doesn't come with us, she doesn't get food."

"Actually, it's not legal to refuse her food. Make sure and bring her tray." *Oh, fudge, I've just been too domineering again and Shelly will hear about it.*

I head towards Enid's room. She is sitting in the chair by her bed, leaning over to Velcro together her tennis-shoe flaps with her right hand. She has on the green sweater and black baggy jeans.

"How do you feel? Your X-rays are negative, but I know it must still hurt. Did the Tylenol help? Are you hungry? Will you come to the day area to eat your supper?" I'm totally ignoring a cardinal rule that says to ask one question at a time.

She answers softly, "I have to tell you something," while she continues looking towards her shoes.

I bend down, my face close to hers. The smell of vanilla is very strong; she is obsessed about that lotion. "What is it, Enid?"

She sits up some so I can see her face more clearly. Her eyes are red and puffy as if she has been crying, but are now dry. "I, um, I didn't really get hit and thrown into the wall," she whispers, "I hurt myself."

I sit down hard onto her bed and stare at her, unbelieving. "What do you mean? How? Why?"

"I just got upset, so I hit myself a bunch of times. I was just mad so I said someone else hurt me."

"But Enid, that just doesn't sound like you." *It doesn't sound possible either.*

From down the hall, a tech is yelling, "Everyone out, closing the doors."

I yell back, "Close them, I'm with Enid."

"Enid, are you afraid of someone? Is that why you're saying this?"

She stands, turning away from me. "Just leave it be. I don't want all this fuss, I shouldn't have ever told you. You're just like all the rest of them."

"OK," I reply, standing too. She's too upset now to pursue this. "Will you come down to eat?"

She abruptly walks out of her room, holding her left arm closely to her chest. I stand and follow her, then come up ahead of her to unlock the doors into the day area. She doesn't allow me eye contact.

Something happened while I was held up in Shelley's office. Something that made Enid think she had to change her story. Something unethical. Something illegal. And, something I can't do a damn thing about.

Patricia Taylor

What She Wanted

T.J.'s mother was lying on her right side, facing sturdy metal side-rails. She had flung off, in her restless state, the natty white blanket and sheet that covered her legs and was trying to flatten the hospital issue pillow that supported her back. Only because her left hand was restrained to the side rail and her right side was paralyzed had she not been able to pull out the plastic tube in her nose into which flowed liquid nourishment. She didn't speak but she moaned and could nod her head when spoken to. I pushed the nurse's button which was on a cord pinned to her faded blue cotton gown: it extended to an intercom on the wall. When the ward clerk's voice asked how she could help me, I asked for our nurse.

Instead of our regularly scheduled nurse, a young bouncy, smiling student nurse entered. She wore her hair in a blond ponytail with a forest green ribbon that matched her uniform.

"Hi, I'm Nan; I'll be here to take care of you today until three." *Much too cheerful for the* situation and she hasn't said a word to T.J.'s mom.

"Hello, I'm Patti, Doris's daughter-in-law. She needs something for pain."

"Let me go check if it's time," she said as she turned and exited the room. *Isn't she going to assess her? Maybe she's just here to give a bath, but why didn't she tell me? Did she already assess her and explain her role to T.J. before I got here?*

I grabbed a cold wet cloth from the bathroom and wiped Doris's sweaty face until Nan returned.

"We gave her a beer a half an hour ago while your husband was here, so it's too early for pain med now," she said, still with that inane smile.

"What? You can see she's hurting. She needs a narcotic." My heart felt like a drum in my chest.

"I already asked my instructor and she says it's too early after the beer."

"I need to see your instructor."

*   *   *

T.J.'s Mother, Doris, had been in the hospital in Alabama for four days before we found out about it. She had been found in her home on the kitchen floor by the police when the rural mail carrier had noticed that she hadn't picked up her mail in several days and her dog was wandering in the road. The carrier called the police and they broke into her home. Doris couldn't speak and didn't have any note on her of who to call in case of emergency so she was in the hospital alone until a nurse there—Doris used to work in that same hospital—recognized her name and notified one of her friends.

The friend, Shirley, called T.J.

"What?" he replied. I stood beside him listening to his side of the conversation.

"How long has this been?" His voice was taking on a panicky sound.

"Oh my God, I thought something was wrong at Christmas but she wouldn't tell me. Kept saying she was fine." He was running his hands through his dark curly hair.

"We'll be there as soon as we can."

When he hung up he told me. "Her cervical cancer came back.

Patricia Taylor

Her whole pelvis is scooped out with cancer. And she had a stroke and fell at home and stayed there several days. They found her with her cats sitting beside her in the kitchen."

"Oh, that's awful. She must be in so much pain," I said, thinking to myself, I've got to call my boss and ask her for time off. This is too much for T.J. to do alone.

"She apparently didn't want anyone to know and was hoping to die at home. I think she's been treating the pain with whiskey," T.J. said.

*   *   *

We got the next flight from Tampa to Birmingham and then rented a car to the small town near where Doris lived and where T.J. was raised. We arrived at the hospital at three am, exhausted but still feeling shock and anxiety too, and went straight to her. She was sitting up in the bed and when she opened her eyes, she immediately recognized T.J. Tears wet her cheeks.

"Mom, can you talk?" he asked, holding her left hand, which held an IV catheter.

She didn't answer, but shook her head slightly, and her tears increased. I knew that people with strokes often cry when they can't express themselves. I sat in a brown hard chair on the other side of the bed and surveyed the room. It was typical with a hospital bed, side tables piled with a phone, TV control, nursing equipment, and two chairs; all in brown. Even the curtains had shades of brown swirls and were closed. There were no flowers or cards. I made a mental note to get something pretty from the gift shop the next day.

T.J. asked. "Mom, are you hurting?" She nodded and he pushed the nurse's button to ask for something for pain.

*   *   *

After a couple hours of sleep, and picking up Doris's two Siamese cats and dog from the neighbor who took them in when she realized what had happened, we returned to the hospital. After checking on Doris, we asked to speak to the primary physician, a Dr. Stone. He arrived a few hours later; a young, handsome— too handsome— man. I didn't trust men that were too good-looking. And, he was immaculately dressed, wearing a suit and tie. He looked more like a lawyer or hospital administrator than a doctor.

We expressed our shock at the extent of her cancer. "Don't blame me," he said, standing close to Doris's room exit door. "Her condition didn't just happen," he added. *Rude much?*

"Of course, "T.J. replied, "But we honestly didn't even know she was sick. We were just here for Christmas three months ago and she never said a word about it."

"Well, she's an elderly woman; you should have kept in closer touch." Before we could respond he added, "There is nothing we can do for the cancer, it's too far gone." But she has a serious infection, so I've consulted an infection specialist, and, as you can see, we are feeding her since she can't swallow. And we can order physical therapy and speech therapy.

We?

"What about pain medicine?" I spoke up. "They've been giving her Demerol shots, can she have something else IV?" Having been a cancer nurse myself, I knew Demerol was not for cancer pain and intramuscular shots were inhumane for chronic pain.

"No, I don't see any reason for that, Demerol should be more than adequate."

I just realized this guy isn't an oncologist, or even a very good doctor.

"Could you consult an oncologist?" I asked.

"No, like I said, there is nothing we can do about the cancer."

"I was thinking for pain control." I was not used to having to be this assertive with a physician. Having worked with really good oncologists, I didn't have to.

T.J. joined the conversation, just as Dr Stone turned to leave. "Can she have beer when she wants it? I know she'd like that, and she has been swallowing liquids."

"Well that's unusual, but you can try if you bring some in for her."

We both murmured our thanks as he left the room.

*   *   *

"What can I help you with? I got your message this morning."

I thought that the patient representative, who called herself Jane, seemed friendly and caring and I was relieved. "Thank you for meeting with us. We are really frustrated," I replied, sitting forward on a lumpy lime- green couch in Jane's office and grabbing T.J.'s hand as he sat beside me.

"Tell me what's going on." She made eye contact; the first person who has done that since we arrived.

"We want to see if we can fire our doctor. We aren't happy at all with the medical care my husband's mother is receiving." I look to T.J. for confirmation and he nods.

"You want to fire your doctor? Have you talked to him about your concerns?"

I thought about how this was very unusual and going to be hard to explain. And normally I would be sitting here letting T.J. do all the talking, but I'm just so angry and sure that this is such a bad situation that I can't keep my mouth shut.

"Have you talked to Dr. Stone?" Jane gently repeated.

I thought, no, I haven't told Dr. Asshole that we want to fire him. But we have tried to say that we don't want aggressive care and he keeps blowing us off and ordering more specialists and therapy, and tube feedings which are just feeding the cancer. "We've told him we don't want aggressive care and it's clear she doesn't want it either, or she would have gone for medical help months ago."

I thought about T.J.'s talk with his mother that morning. He asked her if she wanted to go home with Hospice and stop all her treatments except better pain medication. Doris had looked at him carefully and nodded her head, 'yes.'

We explained to Jane more details regarding her medical care and Doris' expressed desire to go home. Jane said she would talk to Dr. Stone for us, and she would get in touch with us later in the day. We left her office feeling more hopeful, but still not confident that Jane could really help.

*   *   *

However, after we talked to Jane, things moved quickly. Dr. Stone agreed to discharge Doris the next day, and send her home with Hospice care. T.J. explained the plan to his mother and she cried. We followed in the ambulance that took her home and settled her in the hospital bed that we had set up in her living room. It was a large room filled with perfectly cared for antique furniture and had a big picture window that over-looked the lake and woods behind her house. Her peach trees were blooming pink and white flowers, and the grass was becoming a bright green. T.J. put Doris' two huge Siamese cats on her bed and she smiled for the first time. I pulled her feeding tube. We planned for her to have a comfortable, dignified death.

Mimi, her hospice nurse, arrived soon after we got Doris settled. Mimi was a woman in her sixties with graying blond hair, cut very close to her head. She wore navy blue scrubs that highlighted her hazel eyes. She was calm and kind. And we trusted her right sway.

"We need to get her on adequate pain med. I suggest a Dilaudid pump," was the first thing she said after taking Doris's history and doing a gentle physical assessment.

I could have kissed her. "Thank you, that's exactly what she needs." Dilaudid is a serious narcotic that would continually push the drug into her system via a needle placed in her abdomen. They just need to be changed every few days.

"We will start on a low dose and work up depending on how she tolerates it "Mimi said.

I knew it would make Doris sleepy and she would become addicted but that was not a problem we needed to worry about.

We talked more about general care, which I was familiar with, such as the need for Doris to be frequently turned to prevent more skin break down, nutrition as she could tolerate—Mimi didn't mention the missing tube feeding—and bowel care. Another advantage of the narcotic was that it was constipating and Doris had been oozing stool along with urine through a gaping hole in her lower pelvis. It was causing skin irritation and infections. She would also need very frequent diaper changes. Mimi brought in several bags of diapers and bed protector pads from her car along with ointment for skin irritation. She made a trip to the pharmacy after calling the Hospice Doc with recommendations for a Dilaudid pump returned and set up the system.

We decided on a schedule of every hour diaper and position

changes during the day. I set the alarm so we could get up every two hours during the night, so we could turn and change her. When friends would drop by and ask what they could do to help, we asked them to sit with Doris so we could take a nap. One special night, Shirley, Doris's best friend, stayed the evening so T.J. and I could go out to eat steak and French fries at the local Bar and Grill.

At dinner that night we were like giggly children. We felt so free and talked happily about how well everything was going for Doris, and congratulated ourselves on what a good job we were doing. Grief didn't hit us until sometime later.

* * *

Doris lay in the bed in her home with her head elevated and on a silk pillow, covered with a home-made quilt of dogs and cats. Her white, silky shoulder length hair was freshly brushed back off her forehead and over the pillow and she smelled like roses from the lotion we had rubbed into her skin after her bath. Peter, Paul and Mary were singing *Puff the Magic Dragon*. I had a small sip of Old Forester whiskey that tasted like something you'd clean with, but pleasantly burned my throat and chest. I poured an ounce into a Derby shot glass for Doris. She held up her left arm up and wrapped her fingers around the glass and I helped her to a few sips. Her arm dropped, she sighed heavily, and closed her eyes. The constant narcotic was making a big difference for her.

* * *

"Mom, would you like to see Hound Dog?" T.J. asked a week later, referring to Doris's old dog. The cats had been sleeping on her bed and growled every time we made them move to care for Doris. But the dog had been outside and T.J. would go outside to throw a ball to him a few times a day. He was a mutt and about 100 pounds and looked like his name with sad droopy eyes and floppy ears.

Doris replied by nodding, so T.J. brought the dog in on a leash. His bottom end wagged so fast and hard that he knocked several items off the tables on the way to the bed. The cats ran to another room. T.J. held up the dog's front paws on the bed so Doris could pet them with her good hand. Hound Dog licked her face.

"Hound Dog missed you," I said. She didn't acknowledge my presence. She never actually did. She had never liked me and always ignored me when T.J. and I would visit. He said it was because she was attached to his high school girlfriend and had always wanted them to get married. I went to change the record to another *Peter, Paul and Mary* album, which was what T.J. said, was Doris's favorite music.

*   *   *

I fed Doris a few bites of applesauce and mashed potatoes, a couple of her favorite foods, and let her sip a cold Michelob, after we turned her. T.J. went outside to check on Hound Dog. *I'm leaving on a Jet Plane,* was playing on the record player. I sat beside her quietly for a few minutes while she dozed, noticing her breathing was becoming more shallow. Then I took her dish and the beer to the kitchen,

When I returned, she was awake. I started to pull the quilt over her chest and arms. But she reached up to me, smiled, and pulled me down towards her face with her good left arm. She hugged my neck. I froze in her embrace. It was the first and last time she ever really acknowledged me. Then she let go and I covered her, and she relaxed and closed her eyes again.

*　　*　　*

I stepped outside on the back porch and joined T.J. and Hound Dog. The dog sat on T.J.'s feet as he stood to greet me. It was cool and breezy and we wrapped our arms around each other awkwardly with the dog between us; we both starred at the full moon. I was reminded that things always seemed to get more hectic in the hospital when the moon was full; the ER was overcrowded, more babies were born, and all patients on the floor seemed unusually restless. It had been like one long full moon for us the last month. I put my head on T.J.'s warm man-smelling chest and suddenly felt as tired as if I'd been in a marathon. If he hadn't been holding me up, I think I would have collapsed.

"You aren't going to believe this," I started.

"What?" He tensed slightly, probably expecting bad news.

"She gave me a hug." I smiled up at him.

"What brought that on?" he questioned.

"I don't know, I was just tucking her in like usual."

"Well, she probably knows it was you who gave her the death she wanted."

"I don't think it will be much longer, her breathing is changing." He tensed again, and when I looked up his eyes were wet. Then he relaxed, kissing the top of my head. I realized I hadn't washed my hair in days; in fact, I hadn't bathed in days. I could imagine how I looked in my long, greasy hair and old Christmas reindeer flannel pajamas and slippers. But somehow it didn't matter. An owl hooted in the distance. We stood perfectly still.

One Lie Short

"*I* need the red pills."

"I've already given you all your night meds. And you don't get anything red," I reply, sighing.

"I need the red pills."

I'm working night shift, seven pm to seven am. It's a Saturday night, and while the rest of the world is out having fun, it seems, I'm locked in a unit of the state mental hospital with 24 chronically, psychiatrically ill men, ages 18 to 72. And then there are all the hostile mental health techs.

It sounds bleak, or scary, but actually I'm not locked in; after all, I carry the keys. And the techs are hostile on *every* shift. This is actually my favorite time to work. Generally I'm on eleven p.m. to seven a.m., and I rarely see most of the patients except for a brief time in the morning when I'm busy drawing blood work, giving insulin to those who need it before breakfast, and finishing up documentation. I don't often get to chat with patients then.

But every third week, I work a seven-day stretch which includes two twelve-hour shifts on the weekend. And I have from 7 p.m. till bedtime to talk to these men in between all my other duties. They are, for the most part, delightful. After living in this state psychiatric hospital for sometimes months or more, they are appreciative of any attention. These men love for me to watch sports or play cards or just to sit and listen.

Tonight I played rummy with a few of the men, while they

made up their own rules and I lost. Then I gave literally drawers full of anti-psychotic, antidepressant, and anti -seizure meds. I made sure I had plenty of Haldol and Ativan in stock for psychiatric emergencies. It's now eleven o'clock and most of the patients are sleeping. The techs shooed them out of the day room at ten pm, turned off the television, and sent them to bed. One of the techs is carrying a clipboard and checking off patients' whereabouts every fifteen minutes, while the other four techs station themselves around the unit to observe any patients who start to wander.

I'm trying to check all the charts for any doctor's orders that were written that day to make sure nothing was missed. I overhear Della, the head tech, yelling at a patient to get back to bed. *Oh, no, here we go.* I unlock and re-lock the two doors that lead from the nurses' station to the unit. Della, a large, muscular woman, is arguing with Mr. Benjamin. He's standing outside of the waist high circular desk that surrounds the mental health tech observation area where Della stands facing him, hands on hips.

"Della, I'll take care of this," I tell her in as even a voice as I can muster. I know from experience that she hates to be corrected when she is interacting with patients. She and the other techs don't believe the RN has any responsibilities in the direct care of patients except to give the meds. And administration hasn't done anything to give her a different impression.

"He needs to go back to bed, he does this every night just to madden us," she yells at me, while pointing at him.

He doesn't move, but looks expectantly at me.

"Mr. Benjamin wants to talk to me about his medication. Is that right?" I smile at him and he nods.

"If you want to waste your time with him, go ahead." She sits down behind the desk, folding her arms, and glaring at me.

Patricia Taylor

"Thank you, Della," I reply while turning to him." Come with me Mr. Benjamin." I'll pay for this later.

He follows me to the medication room's locked door and we stand outside it in the hall, out of hearing reach of Della.

"What do you need?" As if I don't know.

Mr. Benjamin has a history of paranoid schizophrenia and is now exhibiting dementia. He's waiting on a nursing home bed in his home county. Wearing baggy blue flannel p.j.'s and ratty slippers, with a stooped posture and deep lines in his face and gray stringy hair, he looks much older than his 60 years. I've noticed this in most of our patients. Mental illness is apparently exhausting,

"I need my red pills."

I know not to argue with him, but he has done this every night that I've been with him. He goes to bed, and then gets up about an hour later to ask for his red pills, that have not been prescribed. A few times he's agreed to take Tylenol, and then he's gone back to bed for awhile. But then he gets up and asks for his red pills again. But tonight, he's not accepting Tylenol. So I have a new idea.

"I'll get it in a few minutes," I say, and leave him standing there. I go back to the nurses' station the way I came, past Della who is still glaring at me. Then I find my purse and take out my treat I was saving for later in the night and slip it in my pocket.

I return to the hall, walk past Della and Mr. Benjamin, smiling now, and go into the medication room, unlocking and locking again, and grab a white paper pill cup and cup of water.

When I return to him in the hall, I glance to make sure Della can't see me and hand him the paper cup which contains two red M & M candies and the water. He eagerly takes the cup, and swallows them with water.

And he turns and walks back past the surprised Della in the

nursing station and towards his bedroom down the hall.

It worked. I mentally punch the air over my head.

And then I feel guilt. I am never, ever supposed to lie to a patient. Mrs. T, in nursing school, stressed that. We are supposed to reinforce reality; like if a patient sees little devils with pitchforks flying towards him, you are supposed to say "I don't see them but I know they are real to you." Or in this case, say, "There are no red pills prescribed at this time."

But wouldn't it be neat if I could put my idea on the chart for other nurses to do the same? It would save a lot of stress for the nursing home nurses, and keep Mr. Benjamin happy. But of course, I could never admit to what I just did.

Mr. Benjamin stays in his room and seems to be sleeping well the few times I make my rounds. The techs check every patient every 15 minutes, but I'm not sure they stand there long enough to make sure everyone is breathing. So I check myself every few hours just to make sure, and it always gives me a sense that all is right with the world when I find them breathing deeply and calmly.

*   *   *

I spend the next several hours doing all my routine assigned chores which include lots of paper work, filling and organizing the medications in each patient assigned drawer for the day nurse, defrosting the refrigerator, and restocking equipment; all things that bore me to death. I get excited when I find a patient awake and we can talk a few minutes.

So I walk for awhile with Mr. Burke, who wakes up at three every morning and paces the hall in his pajamas until everyone else is wakened for showers and breakfast. He asks me the same thing every night: Will I contact the FBI to tell them he has been kidnapped and he is here and to come and get him?

"Yes, I'll call them. " What am I going to say? I've already tried to encourage reality by telling him he is a patient here, but when I did, he got very agitated, and walked away, and refused to speak to me for the rest of the night.

"Do you know the number? It is 601 462 7821. Talk to Suzie Underwood. 601 462 7821, 601 462 7821, Suzie Underwood. " He talks very fast and almost in a whisper, looking around to make sure no one else can hear him.

"Yes, I know, I will call her."

"Tell her where I am and to come get me. I have been kidnapped. I am on a special mission." His speech and pace increase and I follow him to the end of the hall and back down the length of it again. When we pass the nursing station and several of the mental health techs, I smile at them, and they roll their eyes and smirk at us.

"Special mission?" I reflect. This is a communication technique, called reflection, which tells the patient you are listening and encourages him to say more.

We pass a poster of the local college football team looking tough in red and white uniforms and helmets. *Talk about an obsession.*

He nods. "I was chosen especially for this. I'm a genius at what I do. I speak 12 languages."

"Wow, what's that like." I inanely ask.

"It's like . . . I'm great." He smiles briefly. "You need to call the FBI and tell them I have been kidnapped and to come get me."

"OK"

"Do you have the number? It's . . . "

When I say goodbye to Mr. Burke, he nods, and continues

pacing in the direction of his bedroom. I wonder how he will function in the group home that has accepted him. He's not a danger to himself or others and his meds are helping as much as they are going to, so he needs to go. I'd be happy for him except that he'll always be so frustrated with his paranoid delusions that are totally real to him.

And I just lied to him. Of course, I'm not going to call that number.

*   *   *

I'm just thinking about having a quick meal break when Della finds me in the nurse's station.

"You better get a shot ready for Mr. Farmer," Della says. She stands over me while I sit at the desk.

"Is he up?" I try to steady my voice and not show that she is intimidating me.

"Yeah, he's up, and he's getting dressed to go to work."

"Oh, brother." *There goes my dinner break again. "* I'll go talk to him."

"Talking's not gonna help. You know what he did last week." She puts a hand on her hip and leans closer to me.

"Yes, I know. But that was because the nurse argued with him. I'm not going to do that."

"He needed a shot then, and he needs one now."

Four nights ago, a nurse was aggressive with him, and he grabbed the nurse. She escaped, ran, and hid behind the enclosed area in the tech observation area. It took calling a code, and everyone running from other units to help restrain him and give him a sedative injection, to prevent the nurse or anyone else from being injured.

Mr. Farmer is in his bedroom wearing jeans and putting on his shoes. About my age, fifty something, he has a large muscular body, dark hair that hangs over his shoulders, a forest green shirt that emphasizes his hazel eyes, and a mischievous smile. I wish that I had met him under different circumstances. Like back before he had a head injury that has severely limited his reasoning.

"Hi, Mr. Farmer," I say as I enter his room.

"Hi," he replies, calmly. He stands up after he has slipped on his high-top sneakers without strings, which are not allowed, and starts pulling out drawers in his bedside table.

"What are you looking for?"

"My keys and wallet. I need to get to work."

"Now?" I hope that doesn't sound like I'm arguing.

"Yes, I have the seven to four shift." I know he worked construction; in fact, that's how he was injured. He fell on his head onto concrete without his helmet. Surgery helped him live but he's lived here ever since.

"Umm . . . You know the doors are locked right now. I'm not sure you can get out anyway." *Now that sounds like arguing.*

"Of course, I can get out. I have to go to work." He stops searching and looks at me with that smile. *Goodness, he's cute. But how am I going to deal with this?*

"Well, OK, let me see if I can find them. I'll look in the nurses' station. Will you wait?"

"I'll come with you, I can't wait long." He follows me out of the room and down the hall.

"You know what? I could drive you. Why don't you sit in the day room a minute and if I can't find your keys, I'll get mine."

"OK, but be quick."

"Oh, I will, just a minute. And how about I get you something to eat to hold you over? Just sit here a minute."

When I find Mr. Farmer in the day room, he is sitting in a hard plastic chair, bolted to the floor, that used to be orange and is now a dirty peach color. He is staring at the empty TV screen, squirming restlessly.

I approach him with a small white paper plate and a cup.

"Here are some graham crackers and juice." I can feel Della's eyes boring into my back. I'm not allowed to offer snacks during the night, and certainly not the juice that is saved for the medication nurse in the morning. I've offered the juice before, because the drinking fountain has not worked since a patient pulled it out of the wall during an angry episode. I was told by the night supervision that patients don't need fluids at night when they are supposed to be sleeping.

They may not need crackers either, but I had some in my bag and I'm going to try this.

"Thank, you, "he replies, taking the plate and cup, and starting to eat vigorously.

In fact, his snack is gone in minutes, and he asks for more. I pull an apple out of my pocket. I hid it there knowing he would ask for more. Patients always ask for more of any little treat they can get.

The apple is gone, again, in minutes and he's sitting back in the chair contentedly, smiling at me.

Mr. Farmer's forgotten all about going to work!

I sit down beside him and ask him what happened in his group therapy yesterday. He's told me before, as have other patients, that they mostly just watch movies.

"Yesterday we saw *King Kong.*"

Really? I can't help but laugh. If only the tax payers knew what they were paying for.

He laughs too.

Patricia Taylor

I'm rushing at the end of the shift to be ready for report for the day nurses when Mr. James approaches me as I pass through the day room. Everyone sits in here in the morning after their baths and waits for time to go downstairs for breakfast. I need to chart the last med I just gave and take the blood work specimens downstairs to go out to a local lab, but here is Mr. James, needing attention now.

Standing too close, he looms over me, with a weird crooked smile and blows stale breath in my face.

"What do you need, Mr. James?" I hope I don't sound as impatient as I feel. I love to talk to patients but the day nurses get so angry when I run late in the morning and I'm starting to feel my 12 hours without a break.

"I need some Tylenol for a headache."

"The doctor said not to give you any Tylenol because your liver enzymes are up."

"Then I want some Milk of Magnesia."

"You aren't constipated."

"Yes, I am"

He's not because I've already seen the list the techs compile of everyone's bowel movements for the night.

"I can't give you anything right now."

He moves even closer to me and stops smiling. "I'm mentally retarded, and mentally ill, and psychotic, and a special student, and have severe pain, and am constipated, and I need medication now."

I am uncharacteristically silent.

I'm saved by Della yelling that the supervisor is on the phone for me.

"I'll be right back," I lie.

"Hello?" I say to the phone.

"I need your blood samples," says the night supervisor.

"Yes, I'm just on my way, Got hung up . . ."

"And a day nurse called in, so I need you to stay another four hours."

"I . . . ."

Darn, why can't I think of a lie now?

The One Who Gets the Hugs

"Tell me what's going on," I gently command as I gingerly approach Sherri. She's pacing the day room. She had just yelled at Lucy, another patient, "Get off the damn phone," and then started to walk. It is dinnertime and only Sherri and Lucy are on the unit, having refused to go to the cafeteria with the other patients.

"I don't care about eating; I'm not hungry." Sherri keeps walking past me, making a circle of the room. I follow at a short distance. There is the smell of burned popcorn in the air. *Must have been the staff; the patients can't use the microwave.*

I walk faster. She's tall to my five foot two so I have to look up to her face when I reach her. "You don't have to eat. I just ordered something in case you get hungry later."

"I'm sick of the food and I'm sick of this place," Sherri replies, huffily. She is wearing a long red fuzzy robe over a T-shirt and jeans. Her red high top sneakers barely peek out under the robe. A wide blue headband holds back her stringy, dirty-blond hair.

"Yes I can imagine you are sick of being here and I can see you're upset. Do you want to sit in the quiet room and talk about it?"

"OK." She turns away from the orange vinyl and wood chairs that all face the television, and heads towards a small room on the right side of the day room that faces the locked medication room on the left. The quiet room is kept empty and used just when patients need to get away from the noise and confusion of the large state psych unit because they are getting anxious. I have needed to sit in it myself more than once. Before we got to the quiet room we passed a large circular four-foot high wall with a locked door the patients are not allowed to enter. It leads into another locked room that is used as the nursing station.

"Do you want a shot to help you calm down?"

I'm so glad she is still in control enough to be able to talk and answer questions. In day shift report the nurse said Sherri had been in her room all afternoon after her mother visited. At dinnertime when we asked everyone to leave their rooms and line up for dinner to go downstairs, she came out but refused to line up. She started pacing when a mental health tech told her she had to go or she would not get any food. I told her she didn't have to go if she didn't want to, but we would bring her food later, as she was obviously getting agitated. The techs weren't pleased but didn't fight it, just gave me nasty looks.

"Yes."

OK, good, she wants the shot which I'm sure will be an anti-psychotic, Haldol, and a sedative, Ativan, that will help her get hold of herself. We pass the medication room on the left and I quickly stick my head in the upper open door and ask Mary, the LPN, to prepare an injection for Sherri. Moving on, we approach the quiet room to our right. When we enter, Sherri sits with her legs crossed under her on the old ,very heavy wooden chair upholstered in vinyl green. I sit near her on the same type of couch. The room has no decorations, no plants, nothing to make it attractive and nothing that anyone could use to harm herself, just like the rest of the unit. The walls are an un-attractive brown yellow. Anyone would feel sick if they were locked in this place. There are no windows, and it's hot and stuffy. There is a screened in porch off the big room, but we have to keep it locked most of the time, for some reason that has not been explained to me.

"Do you want to talk?" I ask softly. I notice how good it feels to sit down a minute. I've only been on shift three hours but my feet are already killing me. I take a deep breath and lean back into the seat while keeping eye contact with Sherri. I wish we had an electric fan but that would be too dangerous. I get a piece of hard candy out of my forest green scrub pocket and hand one to Sherri, which she pops in her mouth. We sit quietly a few minutes tasting sweet peppermint.

"I want another one," she says after a few minutes, holding out her hand.

"That's all I have," I reply. I really don't have another peppermint.

She pouts. "No one cares about me."

"What do you mean?" I ask.

"You don't care and my mother doesn't care," she yells, while starting to rock her body in her chair.

"You don't think anyone cares?" I move over farther away from her on my couch.

"My mother won't take me home." She leans forward over her legs, still rocking, pulling on her greasy hair.

"She will as soon as the team thinks you are ready to go home," I say reasonably, knowing it will probably be awhile until Sherri is ready. She's been in this state hospital for a month and not responding well to medication.

"I'm ready **Now**," she screams as she uncrosses and swings her legs."**Fuck You**."

I stand up and move closer to the door. I realized I've broken a cardinal rule which is not to try to reason with a psychotic person who is upset. I should have just empathized with her feelings. I try again; "You really miss being at home."

"My family doesn't want me back. That's the only reason I'm still here."

I lean against the closed door and wonder where Mary is with the injection. Sherri starts to mumble to herself while she rocks. I can't make out her words but I know it isn't a good sign. I quietly open the door and step back inside the door frame.

"Where are you going? Are you trying to get away from me? I won't hurt you, you know," she says petulantly.

"Oh, I know that, I'm just checking on Mary." I actually don't know that. Sherry's agitation is making me nervous. I leave the room and move down the hall back to the medication room. "Mary, we need the med, like STAT, she's getting really upset."

"I can't find an order for it," Mary replies, searching through her handwritten medication lists. I can see her point, as the records are hard to read, but I don't have time for this now.

"Everyone has a P.R.N. order. She must have one," I reply, feeling really frustrated now.

"I'll go check the chart." She slowly walks past me go to into the walled area around the nurses' station, taking time to lock her door and then unlock two more doors with her keys to get to the medical records. When Mary disappears, I go back to stand outside the room where Sherri sits. I can hear her talking more loudly to herself. I quietly close the door and let her sit alone while *I* pace back and forth in the hall.

I know my supervisor would say that this is the time to call a 'code green.' A code would make every available nurse and mental health tech come running to prevent a dangerous episode. But they would all gang up on Sherri and hold her down and then probably throw her in seclusion or maybe even restraints if she starts to fight, which she probably would. I really hate to do that to her. I want to handle this quietly by ourselves if we can. But we need the injection now.

When I reach the wall around the nursing station, I can see

that the tech, Wanda, has talked Lucy into getting off the phone without incident and they are both watching TV with their backs to me. I hear a silly talk show, one of those ones where people get paid to totally embarrass themselves. I yell to Wanda, "Please come help me." But she doesn't even turn her head my way. They both laugh as two women start to physically fight on the television.

I hear the door to the quiet room open. Then Sherri is rushing towards me. I see her coming but it doesn't register what she is about to do. Her right hand is in the air and balled into a fist. I don't run sideways or put up my hands to ward off a blow as I've been taught. I back up to the rounded wall surrounding the outer part of the nurse's station. She hits me with her fist several times on the top of my head. I yell out with surprise but don't move or try to protect myself in any way. I feel an intense sharp pain in my head and my eyes start to water.

Wanda hears me and finally runs over to pull Sherri away from me. I help her lead Sherri into the quiet room just as Mary runs into the med room again, calling out "I'm getting it." I hold Sherri by one arm as Wanda holds her around her waist. I can barely hold Sherri but Wanda is a large strong woman and has no trouble restraining her while we wait for Mary. Sherri is yelling and cussing at us and trying to break free. She's past being able to think about the fact that she wanted the shot a short time ago.

When Mary enters with the injection, Wanda holds Sherri while facing her, while I grab Sherri's red robe, hold it back, and pull down her jeans on one side just a short way. Mary quickly finds a safe spot, cleans it with alcohol, and injects the medication into her large hip muscle. We adjust Sherri's clothes and walk her to the chair she had been sitting in. She stops fighting us and curls into a ball in the chair, crying loudly now. "You bitches," she whines.

"We needed to do that to help you relax. I'm sorry we had to hold you," I say unhelpfully.

We leave her alone with the door closed and the overhead lights off to decrease stimulation. I can still see her through the small window in the door. I stand there watching Sherri for what seems like forever until it's obvious she's slumped in a chair and obviously getting sleepy. I run my hands over my head, feeling a lump rising on the top of my head.

I then walk over to remind Wanda to check on Sherri every 15 minutes. I'm afraid she won't really do this, as there is a good chance she'll forget while she is watching TV. She's not supposed to be watching TV but that's a battle I'm not going to win.

I go to the nurses' station to document in detail everything that just happened with Sherri. Then I call the supervisor and fill out an incident report regarding my attack. The supervisor gives me a hard time for not calling for help sooner and not getting out of Sherri's way. "You should not put people in danger like that." I can feel a major pain setting in all over my head.

The next afternoon I show up for work still in pain and well aware that I chose to freeze instead of fly when the sympathetic nervous system kicked in. I wonder, not for the first time, if I'm cut out to be a psychiatric nurse in a state institution. But then when they see me, many of the patients rush towards me to beg for their daily hug and tell me all their concerns and complaints about the day. They cry or laugh and tease me about the cowlick that always sticks up on my head. One woman calls me a chick-a dee. I give quick hugs and say I'll be back to talk to them after I get report.

Later after I've assessed almost everyone on the unit and listened briefly to everyone who wants to talk, Sherri approaches me.

She has obviously washed her hair and taken off the red robe. She's pretty in a blue and green cotton top and clean jeans. "Aren't you going to hug me?"

I stand back a little, and reach for my throbbing head.

"I'm not going to hurt you," she insists.

"The last time you said that you ended up hitting me." Definitely not therapeutic, but it just came out of my mouth.

"Just a little hug."

I open my arms and reach up to her, and give a tentative hug.

Then I remember that the reason I wanted to be a nurse. It was so I could be the one to give and get the hugs. So I hold on tighter and she holds me back.

Photo: Amanda Nolin

Tricia Taylor based these mostly fictional short stories on over 40 years of nursing experience in four southern states in the U.S. She received her BSN, RN at FSU in 1976, and MSN at USM, in psychiatric nursing, in 1992. Her experiences included cancer nursing, hospice, med-surg, pediatrics, newborn nursery, teaching psychiatric nursing in a nursing program for twenty years, and then a return to med -surg, ER, quality control nursing, and finally psychiatric nursing, until her recent retirement. This collection highlights a career that was usually exhausting, sometimes tragic, frequently infuriating, occasionally funny, and consistently rewarding. She now lives with her husband Joe Taylor, writer and publisher, and 11 rescue pets in rural Alabama.